Punch Drunk Kisses

Alan Cowsill

About the Author

Alan Cowsill has worked as a writer and editor for Marvel UK/Panini and Eaglemoss Publishing. He created the award-winning *Classic Marvel Figurine Collection* and *DC Super Hero Collection* and worked on the *Marvel Chess Collection* and *Marvel Movie Collection*. His books include *Colin the Goblin, Stormwatcher, DC Comics: A Year by Year Visual Chronicle, Marvel Comics: 75 Years of Comic Art, Spider-Man Chronicle, Marvel Avengers Character Encyclopedia* and the award-winning graphic novel *World War One* (Campfire, 2014). He was also one of the writers of *Revolutionary War* for Marvel. He is presently the Managing Director of Bullpen Productions.

For updates, news of future releases, behind-the-scenes secrets of *Punch Drunk Kisses* and more, join the mailing list. Email: "PDK Mailing List" to
alancowsill@gmail.com

We need your help too. If you enjoyed this book please leave a quick review on Amazon or whichever platform or online store you bought it from.

Published by Bullpen Productions

Contact: alancowsill@gmail.com

Website: alancowsill.com

www.bullpenproductions.co.uk

ISBN: 978-0-9956994-0-3

Cover artwork by Paul Morris

www.mostlygreenstuff.com

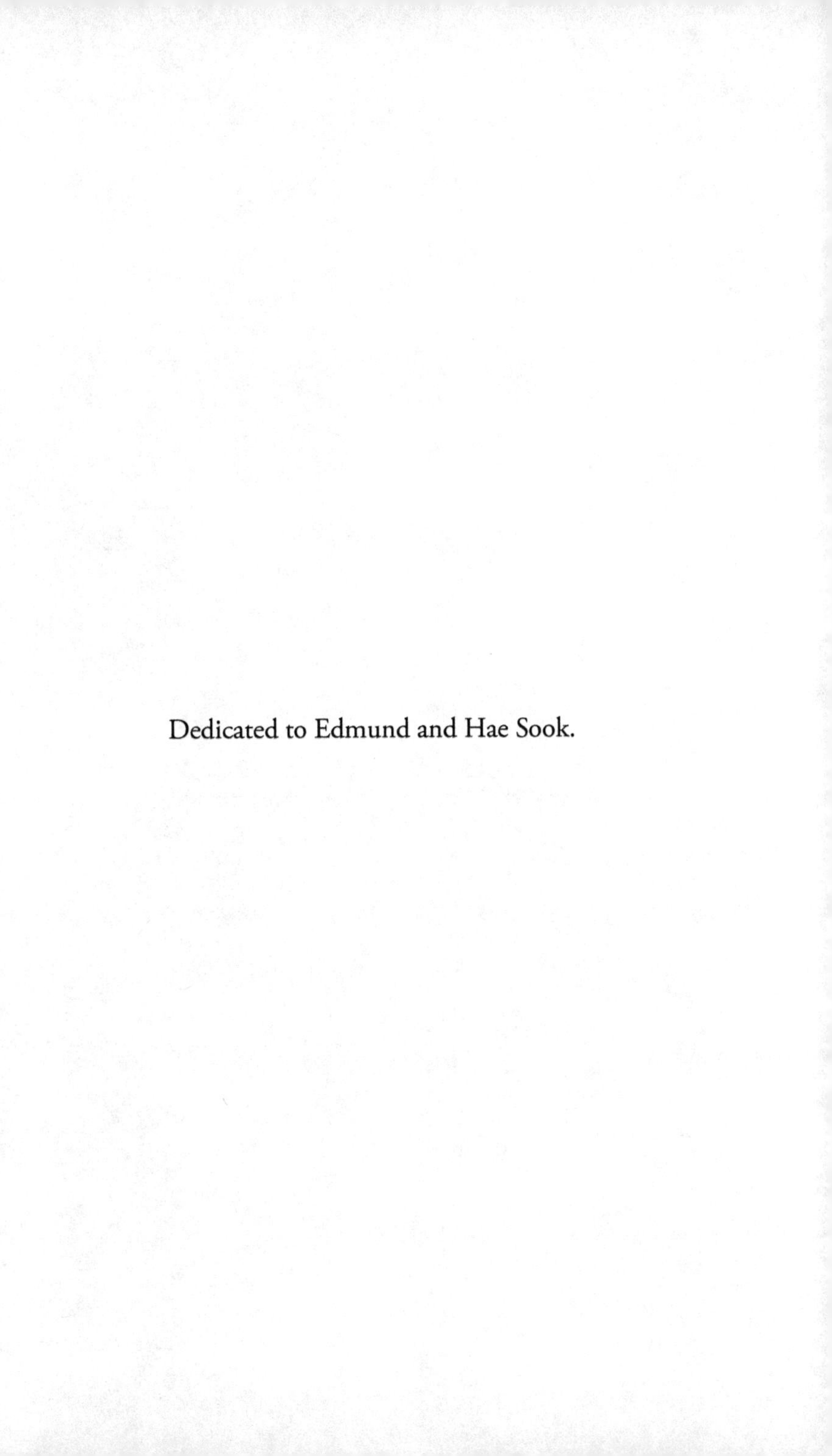

Dedicated to Edmund and Hae Sook.

One

Balls, Penguin Racing and Matters of the Heart

Once upon a time, twenty-two Northerners were playing football on a wet and miserable Sunday morning. Despite the hangover and the taste of stale kebab loitering in my mouth, I was defending for the Hope and Anchor, my local, against the Greyhound. Not only were the Greyhound our bitter rivals but my mortal enemy, Jez Bullion, played for them. They were top of the league and winning twelve-nil.

The name's William Cade, I'm twenty-six and what follows is the truth, the whole truth and nothing but the truth. Only the names have been changed to protect the guilty.

"Charlie," I yelled, as the ball was belted towards a fellow defender. "Put the fag out and concentrate on the game!"

The phrase "lanky streak of piss" had been specifically created with Charlie Stringer in mind. He was thirty-five going on sixty, with thinning, greasy, black hair and the fixed expression you usually find on a starving weasel caught in the headlights of a truck. I watched with mild amusement as he threw his fag to the ground and ran towards the ball. He closed his eyes as he leapt towards it, arms flailing wildly like a blind penguin on crack. The ball bounced off his head straight to my good self.

A deep ball into the Hope's defence by the Greyhound, my internal sports commentator cut in. *Stringer's lost it but Cade's moving up, he'll have that one covered. Yes, it's the old Cade special. A beautiful clearance that takes the ball safely up the field. He really is the star of the team and he's...*

The commentary was ended abruptly when one of their players knocked me back to reality and straight into a muddy puddle.

"Sorry, mate. I was a little late," a familiar voice mocked.

Jez Bullion. The first person I ever got into a fight with. Bastard nicked my football when I was five. We used to fight all the time. I think he was jealous of my good looks and happy home life. His was fucked. Mrs Bullion used to shag anything and everything that moved while his dad got pissed at the pub and then tried to beat them all up. My home life was fine – at least until Jenny, the divorce and my mother's discovery of cheap wine.

I was about to react when John intervened.

"Leave it, Billy. You'll only get sent off again," he shouted, blocking my path to Jez.

I breathed slowly and decided to do just that. Partly because John was my mate but mostly because he was three times my size. His full name was John Wayne and, as well as being our team captain, he was the landlord of the Hope and Anchor. He did look a little like the other John Wayne too, albeit in a big, beer-bellied, Northern way. His mother, Annie, was a big Western fan. John's kid brother was called Lee – middle name Van. Local legend has it that his mum had prayed for a third son when she first saw *A Fistful of Dollars*, but God had intervened and allowed her husband to shack up with a seventeen-year-old trapeze artist from Wigan rather than inflict Clint Wayne on the world.

"I'm good," I lied, as both John and Jez ran back up the field, where we'd somehow managed to get a corner. Feeling like a change of scene, I jogged up to the halfway line and watched the corner as it came in… and bounced off one of our players into the back of the net. The team went crazy – it was our first goal in six games.

"You do know you're still losing by eleven goals?" the referee said as we prepared to restart the match.

"Sure," I grinned. "But we've scored. Probably the start of a comeback."

For the next ten minutes, we played like champions. Okay, maybe not champions but we did manage to stop them scoring another goal. I was especially pleased as Jez and his tit of a mate Geoff hadn't had a look-in for the whole game. Okay, so it felt like running around had cost me my entire respiratory system but I never used it much and it was worth it just to fuck up their day.

"Billy, heads up!" Lee shouted.

Here comes their number six, the Cade commentary started again after a long commercial break. *This guy's had trials with Wigan and is by far their best player, but judging by the way Cade's played today, he'll be more than equipped to stop him.*

I did my best to go for the ball. Honest. It was just all the rain made it very hard to do anything properly, especially a sliding tackle, so it wasn't really my fault when instead of getting the ball I sent him flying through the air.

The ref blew his whistle.

"I'm sorry," I said to the player, helping him to his feet. And I really was. Partly because it had been a nasty tackle but mostly because his brother was known as Big Mac, a giant psychopath of a man who was very protective of his little brother – and had clearly taken umbrage at my actions.

"Nice stop," John said. "Now get in the wall."

Charlie and a couple of other guys were already standing in line – each looking a bit worried as Big Mac lined up the free kick.

"I can't," I told John. "Mac wants to kill me."

"Mac is a professional. He'll go for the shot. Now do as you're told and get in the bloody wall."

As I joined the others, Mac smiled at me. It was the sort of smile Hannibal Lecter used when feeling peckish. As it was Sunday, I decided a quick prayer was in order.

Our Father, who art in Heaven, if the Lord is with me, forgive us our tackles and protect my balls from those who would trespass against them.

I was about to add "At the hour of our death", when Mac took the free kick and everything went black…

"Billy?"

Voices. Laughter. Pain.

I opened my eyes to see the ref and a few players leaning over me.

"Is he alive?" Charlie asked.

"Don't know," Lee said. "Never seen anyone stop a shot like that."

"Did they score?" I stuttered, as John helped me to my feet.

"Nah, your balls got in the way," Lee said. "They did get a corner though."

"Billy, take the far post and watch out for Bullion, he's just behind you."

Still dazed, I hobbled to the goal and glanced behind me. Bullion was waiting for the ball, edging closer and closer to me. We started jostling for position. It was quite friendly at first but soon deteriorated into some kind of amateur wrestling bout. As the ball came in, I tried to get some additional height by elbowing Jez in the guts. It was one of my special moves, only this time he got in first and elbowed me. Winded, I collapsed to the ground, opening my eyes just long enough to see him score goal number thirteen. More mud rushed into my mouth. Every part of my body was starting to hurt and I was convinced a heart attack was only seconds away.

No one had told me it would end like this, I thought, deciding to stay there until it was time to go to the pub. Barry, our goalkeeper, had other ideas.

"Come on, Billy. Not long left," he said, helping me to my feet.

Luckily he was right. A few seconds later the ref blew the final whistle and there was peace in our time. Right on cue, it stopped raining and the sun came out.

"Not a bad game," Charlie said, as we left the pitch.

"It was a shite game," John snapped, hurling the ball at Charlie's head. "We were shite, the weather was shite and most of all you were shite even by your own shite standards."

Charlie rubbed his head, looking like a sad puppy left out in the rain. Albeit a very ugly sad puppy.

The funny thing was, Charlie was right. It *had* been one of our better games.

"So," Lee asked. "You split up with whatshername yet?"

The two of us were tailing the team as we headed back to The Hope for the traditional post-match piss-up. "Whatshername" was Lee's pet name for my girlfriend, Pam.

"Not yet," I admitted as we neared the pub. "Things keep getting in the way."

"Yeah, I remember," Lee smiled. "They used to get in the way when I knew her. But tits aren't everything – even big ones."

"That's not what I meant," I replied, refusing to admit to anyone, especially myself, that he might have a point. "It's just that she really seems to like me and I don't want to hurt her. It could crush her."

"Yeah, 'cause no woman in her right mind could get over you, could they?" Lee laughed, shaking his head. "You're a regular hero, having sex with her all the time. Especially considering that thing she does with her…"

"Okay, if you must know I'm doing it today. I promised Jimmy."

Lee started to look uncomfortable. Jimmy was my best friend

and gay. While Lee wasn't a bigot, there were some things he just wasn't programmed to deal with – and Jimmy was definitely one of them. Lee was saved from further embarrassment by Charlie running out of the pub, his insane other half, Lil, close behind and threatening to kill him. It was a regular occurrence.

"See you next week," he mumbled.

"Could be worse," Lee said after they'd gone. "You could be shagging Lil."

"I'd never get that drunk. Is Charlie okay now?"

"Yeah, apparently his testicle's all healed up. Brings tears to my eyes just thinking about it. Poor bastard. You'll never get me under the thumb like that."

I was about to say something but decided against it. Lee and his brother, John, were two of the biggest psychos my hometown had ever produced. They were both ex-squaddies and had served in the Middle East. In fact Lee claimed it was the chemicals over there that made him lose all his hair. Despite his hard-man image, Lee was a bit of a big softy and had been in love with Chrissie, the Hope's barmaid, for as long as anyone could remember.

"Usual?" I asked, as we stepped through the Hope's huge double doors into bedlam.

The Greyhound might have been better than us at football but when it came to drinking, the Hope was in a league of its own.

Both teams were in the bar, complete with friends, match officials and a few students and regulars – including Mad Tommy, the resident drunk. Tommy looked a little like a dishevelled Jimmy Stewart in *Harvey* – only without the giant invisible rabbit. Not that we'd have been able to see an invisible rabbit. Tommy was preparing himself for a Penguin Race, a couple of locals moving two tables back to back to make the track. For those who've never had the pleasure, Penguin Racing involves two or more athletes dropping their trousers round their ankles and running around the connected tables as quickly as possible. When I started drinking in the Hope such things freaked me out a little. Now I was kind of used to them. John said they added ambience. I wasn't so sure but also thought it was important not to argue with someone trained to kill.

Tommy was the world champion of Penguin Racing and raring to go. This time he was pitted against two young – and very drunk – students who had been enticed into the pub by John's reasonable prices. They were young and fit, but didn't stand a chance against Tommy and were soon losing pants down.

"Hey, John," Lee shouted, beckoning his brother over and ordering another round. "Want to hear something funny – Billy's going to dump Pam tonight."

"I thought you'd done that last week?" Chrissie interrupted.

"Got distracted," I said.

"Our Lee used to get distracted all the time when he went out with her," John said. "I'll give you a tip, next time don't stare at her tits."

Chrissie slapped him over the head playfully, John feigning innocence before adding, "Anyway, no time like the present…"

"You've got me a present?" a familiar voice said from behind me.

I got a sinking feeling on hearing Pam's voice. All things considered, that probably wasn't a good sign for the future of the relationship.

"We were just talking about you, weren't we, Billy?" Lee grinned.

"Really?" Pam smiled.

There was a long pause.

Do it, my internal voice said. *Do it now.*

"Nothing important," I eventually said, much to the groans and headshakes of my so-called friends.

"I saw the ghost again last night," Pam said, pecking me on the cheek and sitting by the bar as I got her a drink.

Lee and John melted away.

Did I mention that Pam was a born-again hippy? Albeit one caked in make-up, fake tan, drawn-on eyebrows and really scary-looking false nails.

I downed my Jack and Coke quickly, Chrissie sympathetically replacing it with a double.

"I was lying in bed. It was late – about one in the morning – and all of a sudden the room got really cold – like spiritually cold – and then I saw her, the little girl. She was just standing there, looking really sad and lonely. I was wondering if I should get your mum to do a séance again. After all, the last one nearly worked."

"It's just your imagination," I said, a little too harshly.

"That's just like a Leo, that is, stubborn," she continued. "You have to believe in something. Otherwise what's the point?"

"There isn't one," I said, finishing my drink and feeling my bitterness start to rise. "It's like that tarot you do and fong sui, it's all bollocks."

"Feng shui," John interrupted. "And there's something in

that. Had one of those experts in to look over the pub and the takings shot up."

Lee and I looked at John.

A couple of kids tried to move one of the house plants near the window.

"Oi, put that back, you're ruining the psychic harmony of the establishment!" John shouted, then added to the rest of us, "It was just for a laugh, like."

"You should be more open-minded," Pam told me. "Your mum is. She's got the gift."

"Only when she's pissed," I snapped, feeling guilty as soon as the words left my mouth.

I heard an annoying laugh from behind me and turned to see Jez standing there waiting to order a drink.

"Sorry to hear about your mum," he said, with mock concern. "Saw her earlier. Looked like she'd already had a few. Must be hard having such a…"

Before I could interrupt Jez, John jumped in with a single word. "Careful."

The tone of John's voice was enough to scare anyone – especially someone like Jez – who stepped back straight into Mad Tommy, just as Tommy was about to win the race. Both collapsed on the floor in a heap, one of the young students waddling past to win the race.

"Watch where you're going, you old fart," Jez snapped, pushing himself up. "Take a look, Cade. That's you in a few years' time. Just like your mother, a complete and utter…"

"I think you should leave now," John said.

For a second it looked like Jez was going to do something

stupid. Luckily his friend Geoff saw what was happening and dragged him out of the pub, Jez giving a table near the door a petulant kick for good measure.

Meanwhile, back in the Penguin Race, Tommy was not handling defeat well and was close to tears.

"I lost," he sniffed, as I helped him to his feet.

"I think you'll find the race was abandoned," I said. "Isn't that right, John?"

"But I won," the student said.

"If you consult the slow-motion replay, you'll notice that the race was indeed abandoned and will have to be rerun. If you have any complaints I suggest you take them up with the adjudicator," John explained.

"Oh yeah, and who's that?" the student asked.

"Me," John grinned, looking down at him.

"Oh," the kid whimpered. "In that case, I think you're right."

"Good lad," John smiled, slapping the teenager on the back. "And the next round's on the house."

In case you're worried, Mad Tommy won the rematch.

Time passes quickly in the Hope. Before I knew what was happening it was late and I was outside Pam's flat, steadying myself against the wall as she opened the front door. She'd been quiet all day.

You're going to have sex with her again! My internal voice shouted. *After you said you'd split up with her, as well.*

She turned and smiled at me. She wasn't that bad, all things considered. There was just no emotion there on my part. I wasn't sure there ever had been. It wasn't right. It was time to end it.

"Pam…" I started to slur, pushing myself away from the wall only to fall straight into the garden and smash one of her gnomes.

I stared at the grass for a moment and then went back to the matter at hand.

"Pam, I… when did you get so small?"

"You're talking to a gnome," she said from above me. "One that you didn't manage to break."

I somehow managed to stagger to my feet and held out the smashed shards of her garden ornament.

"That gnome's just like our relationship," she sniffed.

I looked down at the broken pieces and tried to work out what she meant.

"There's something I need to say," I mumbled.

"This just isn't working," Pam sobbed.

"I broke your gnome," I explained.

"Listen," she said. "I don't think we should see each other any more."

"Okay," I replied. "You'll need some cement."

"What?"

"To fix the gnome. I think you'll need some cement."

"Did you hear what I just said?" she asked.

I glanced up and probably looked confused and very drunk. It happens.

"I said we should split up. We can still be friends. I just don't see this working out. Are you going to be alright?"

I carefully placed the pieces of gnome on to the grass and smiled.

"What will you do now?" she asked.

"Probably get a kebab," I answered, staggering off into the night.

As it was, I had the House Special to celebrate my newfound freedom. The grease and pita bread improved my spirits no end. I was singing an old song of Jimmy's and feeling very mellow by the time I reached my house. Pam was already a million miles away, boxed up and filed away in the do-not-open part of my subconscious. I turned and looked back at the road I'd lived in all my life. It was a good street. About a dozen or so semi-detached houses with large gardens at the front and back and old oaks lining the road. The smell of bad eggs drifted over from the glass factory nearby but the stars were out and the moon was full. As I opened the front door, Happy bounded out to meet me. He was such a cool dog and amazingly friendly – especially to people with bits of kebab meat still in their hands. Inside, my mum had passed out on the couch, a couple of empty bottles of wine by her side. One had stained the carpet red. The table was set for two, the candles burnt out. Her latest bloke was supposed to have come around for dinner. It didn't take a detective to work out he hadn't shown. The worst thing about Jez's insults earlier had been the truth behind them. Over the last few years, my mum had started hitting the bottle pretty hard.

But she had her reasons.

We all did.

"Come on," I whispered. "It's time to go to bed."

I helped her to sit up and her eyes half opened.

"Billy… is that you? Did you have a good time?"

"Yeah. It was great. Come on, it's late."

"Your dad called earlier. Said he wasn't going to pay any more… ali… ali… to give me any more money. He said some really cruel things."

I managed to get her standing and she looked straight into my eyes.

"He said I was a dried-out, drunken hag. You don't think I'm a dried-out, drunken hag, do you?"

"No, you're great. It's just Dad. You know what he gets like sometimes."

"You're a good son. Been good to me since Jenny died. She would have been fourteen next month."

"I know, but you can't dwell on it. She's gone now. We've got to carry on. It's what she'd have wanted."

"I know, but it's so hard sometimes. So hard, and she was so pretty."

I looked at the photo by the side of the TV. Mum, Dad, Jenny and myself at the seaside six years ago. Jenny was laughing at something. I couldn't remember what. I remembered Pam's words earlier – that there had to be more to life than this. I hoped she was right. That my sister was in a heaven somewhere and one day I'd get to meet her again, but then I remembered what she looked like, dying in hospital from leukaemia. There was no God and if there was I didn't want to meet him because he'd let my kid sister die and I'd hate him forever for that. There was no point to her death. No grand design. I'd lost a sister and none of us had ever really recovered.

"You're a good son," Mum whispered again as I helped her up the stairs. "Not like your father at all, more like your grandfather. He was a good man. Do you remember him?"

"Yeah," I lied, opening the door to her bedroom with my foot.

When I was a child it seemed to be a perfect place of safety. I'd wander in, scared or sick, and my parents would always take care of me. They'd make everything right. Make the fear go away.

Now the room was cold and full of ghosts.

"He was such a nice man," she whispered, drifting off into sleep.

I let the dog out for a last run and decided to call it a night.

There was no sleep though.

Just thoughts of Jenny.

Two

Sleep, Friends and Shocks

3.33am.

Why couldn't I sleep?

It was late. I was going to feel like shit in the morning.

You already feel like shit, my ever-helpful internal voice piped up.

Yeah, thanks for the insight.

It's the alcohol. Serves you right.

I didn't drink that much.

Yeah, right, this is yourself you're talking to.

Well, I didn't.

You're a fucking alcoholic.

I'm not an alcoholic, I'm just a Northerner. We all drink a lot.

Tell that to your kidneys.

I think they're asleep.

And shouldn't you get a proper job? You can't live on the cash your grandfather left you forever.

I have a proper job.

Serving in the Hope and Anchor is not a proper job. It's a one-way ticket to ending up a big fat loser. Oh, hold on, you are a big fat loser – too late.

I'm not fat.

Right, so that big load of flab around your gut is just pizza retention.

It doesn't seem to damage my chances with the opposite sex.

Have you seen some of the women you've pulled recently?

Not with the lights on.

Very funny.

Yeah, I'm a regular comedian. Now shut the fuck up and let me go to sleep.

I rolled over in bed and placed one of the pillows over my head.

It almost worked.

That was some grey hair the other day.

It wasn't a grey hair, it was just some kind of oddball mutant hair.

You're going grey. You'll be old and fat before you know it.

I got out of bed and looked at my reflection in the mirror.

It wasn't a pretty sight. My shoulders were sagging, my belly flopping out, my chest non-existent… And there it was…

See, I told you so, another grey hair.

I moved to pull it out.

No point trying to do that, it's brought some friends with it. Yup, looks like the grey hairs are about to take over your head – that is if it doesn't all fall out first through your lack of vitamins.

I take loads of vitamins.

Guinness doesn't count.

Does too. The adverts say it's good for you.

Only if you're an alcoholic.

Listen, I'm not an alcoholic, drinking just helps me relax.

Your mum's an alcoholic. Maybe it's in the blood. She's not looking well either. If she doesn't stop drinking soon, she's going to die. Just like your dad nearly died. Remember that heart attack he had?

It wasn't a heart attack, it was just indigestion.

Didn't stop him running to hospital though, did it? Wasn't that the last time you saw him as well?

No, I saw him when he got out of hospital.

Right, and when was that exactly?

Don't know. May sometime?

And it's now almost December. You're not a very good son, are you?

For a while, my internal discussion group must've dozed off. I started to think about ways of allowing sleep to come back. The secret was clearing my mind. If I could clear my mind, sleep would pay me a visit.

Nothing. I had to think about nothing.

…

Nothing.

…

That was it. I was doing it. I was thinking about nothing.

Oh shit, hold on. I'd been thinking about thinking about nothing which meant I'd been thinking about thinking about nothing rather than just thinking about nothing. I'd have to try again.

No. It's no good. My mind's too busy thinking now to think

about nothing. Maybe if I counted to ten really slowly, it'd help me sleep.

One…

Two…

So far, so good, I'm starting to feel really drowsy.

Stop. Concentrate on the breathing and the numbers.

Three…

Four…

Five…

Six…

Seven…

Eight…

Jenny.

Sometimes, I'd wake up and see her standing by the side of my bed. It wasn't her though, and it wasn't a ghost. It was just a memory.

It didn't seem like five years since she'd died.

It didn't…

One Christmas, she gave me this present. It was a woollen hat. She'd spent weeks at school working on the thing. It was the ugliest hat I'd ever seen in my life. There was no way it would fit and I was worried that if I so much as touched it, the whole thing would fall apart. I still have it somewhere. It's beautiful.

An image of Jenny lying in a hospital bed came into my mind without permission. She looked like a shell. A small and broken angel wasting away.

She shouldn't have died.

"She *shouldn't* have died," I whispered, hitting the pillow a few times as though sleep was hiding behind it.

Jenny.

I turned the light on. There was no way I could sleep now. Maybe I'd never sleep again. I'd read somewhere about people who had a medical complaint that prevented them sleeping. They stayed awake constantly until they went mad.

I walked around the bedroom. Near the bookcase was a little pink porcelain cat. Jenny had won it in an arcade on a day trip to Southport a few months before…

She'd handed it to me, kissing my cheek, saying it was for her favourite brother.

I picked it up and tried to recapture her essence. Her hands had touched this. She was gone, but…

I went back to bed and stared at the ceiling. Somewhere along the way, sleep came, because when the phone started ringing it was eight in the morning.

"Hello?" I answered, startled by the sudden burst of my ring tone. "Whole Lotta Rosie (Live)" by AC/DC, in case you're interested.

There was an echo on the other end of the line. Some breathing.

"Jimmy?" I asked, seeing my friend's name on the screen.

"Sorry, I shouldn't have called," his voice said. "It's late or early. I didn't realise how…"

"Jimmy?" I said, scared by how down he sounded. "What's wrong, where are you?"

"Hospital," he answered. "It's Phil. He tried to kill himself."

I was silent for a few moments. Jimmy had been going through a period of dating skinhead loser types and the latest was by far the worst of them.

"Which hospital?" I asked.

"Summerdale," he answered. "It's okay, I don't need anyone here, it's just…"

"Wait there, I'll call a cab."

"There's no need."

"Too late. Done. I was up anyway."

Jimmy was silent for a few moments before saying just one word.

"Thanks."

The receiver went dead. I called a cab.

It took me forever to get to the hospital. I had to pause outside for a few moments and try to put all thoughts of Jenny behind me. She'd died at a hospital on the other side of town, but the smells and appearance of this one were too close for comfort.

It was Monday morning, but not that many people were in A&E. Only half a dozen or so, with potential broken bones and nasty-looking cuts. Most seemed more tired than injured.

I glanced around but couldn't see Jimmy. A voice called out to me as I was about to talk to the receptionist.

"William, is everything alright?"

"Dad?"

He'd just left one of the wards with his new wife, Doris, next to him.

It looked like both of them had been crying. My dad didn't like emotion and tried to avoid it at all costs. At least since Jenny died. My spider-sense went to Def-Con One.

"Billy. We were just talking about you," Doris smiled, sniffing back tears.

My dad stepped forward and hugged me.

"What are you doing here, your mother's okay, isn't she?" he asked, wiping a tear from his eye.

"Mum's fine. It's Jimmy – or rather his boyfriend…" I stopped in mid-sentence.

As a born-again Protestant, Dad had developed a rather bad view of Jimmy over the last few years.

"I thought I saw him," Dad said. "He's grown into a good man, I bet his mother's really proud of him."

"They always are," Doris smiled, stepping forward and sliding an arm through my dad's.

I used to be so close to my dad before everything changed. When I was a kid, the only time I remember not liking him was when he stopped me beating up Jez. He even used to be funny. That changed with Jenny… moving on. My mum discovered drinking and my dad discovered God. He'd met his new wife, Doris, at a church function a year or so after the divorce. She'd started cooking him dinner and before anyone knew what was happening, we all had a wedding invitation. Mum didn't go. She went to her sister's and cried all afternoon.

Watching your dad remarry has to be one of the weirder ways to spend a Saturday. Since then, the new couple had become pretty much self-contained and I hardly ever bothered to visit, even though they only lived a few streets away.

"Is everything okay – it's not your heart again is it?" I asked, my words sending them both into a fit of the giggles.

"No, everything's fine," my dad grinned. "In fact, things couldn't be better."

"You should tell him," Doris giggled. "Why wait until later?"

"You're right – as always," Dad said, pecking her on the cheek before turning his attention to me.

An explanation for their oddly emotional behaviour appeared at the back of my mind but I chose to ignore it on the grounds that it was completely fucking insane.

"We were a little scared earlier about…" Dad paused for a moment and stared at the clock on the wall, his shoes, Doris, before turning his attention back to me. "Doris had an early appointment to check everything was alright with the… well, you see, son, we've got something to tell you."

My dad placed a hand on my right shoulder.

"Doris is expecting," he smiled.

I stared at him blankly. Not quite understanding the sounds coming from his mouth.

"Expecting what?" I mumbled.

"A baby," he grinned. "She's having a baby."

"But she's nearly forty," I mumbled again, beginning to think I was still asleep and this was all some crazy dream.

"Don't look so surprised, son. Your old man's still got what it takes. And we've been trying for ages."

"Are you okay, William? You look a little pale," Doris whispered.

"I don't understand…" I murmured, looking at my dad. He had lots of grey hair. "You can't have a baby. You're… you're… I'm twenty-six and you're…"

"Fifty-five next June. But a young fifty-five. It's just as I've always told you, plenty of exercise, a firm belief in God's love and a decent bowel movement once a day are all you need for a long and happy life."

He turned to smile at Doris.

"Of course, the love of a good woman helps."

The thought entered my head that if she was pregnant, it meant her and Dad had been… intimate. The image of them both at it flashed into my mind without permission and refused to leave. I could almost see her pale, thin, corpse-like body with my dad's sweaty carcass on top of her…

Sweet God in Heaven!

"Are you sure you don't want us to get a doctor or something, William? You look terrible," Doris said.

"When?" I somehow managed to ask.

"May," my father answered.

"I don't know what to say," I said.

It was true. I didn't.

My dad laughed out loud.

"Never mind, son, you'll have a few months to get used to the idea. Now go and see your friend. It sounds like he might need you."

I looked at them both for a moment, not sure what to do.

"Congratulations," I said, shaking my dad by the hand.

Without warning he hugged me.

"I hope it's a girl," he whispered, his eyes starting to cloud over.

I eventually found Jimmy outside the hospital smoking a spliff. He looked terrible. Not stoned but hollow and shaken. I called out his name but he didn't hear me.

"Jimmy?" I repeated, moving in front of him.

He stared at me blankly for a few seconds and then tried to

smile.

"Thanks for coming. I know you're not Phil's biggest fan. It's just… What's wrong? You look white as a ghost."

"I'm fine. How is he?" I asked, not really caring. My thoughts were still running over my own news.

"Okay. They're keeping him in for the day to check him out. Apparently he was doing loads of drugs…"

"Are you okay?"

"Yeah," Jimmy said, stubbing out his spliff. "Better off without him and all that. You know he was up for GBH? I only found out last night. He was getting hassled outside a club in Manchester a few months ago and went crazy. Attacked a bouncer and some poor sod who was trying to calm things down. I knew he was violent but…" Jimmy relit his spliff and inhaled before continuing. "Last night, I'd just finished a gig and went back to his. I'd had enough and didn't want to see him any more. I was going to call him but thought I should be a man and do it face to face. Big mistake. As soon as I told him, he fell dead silent and walked straight into the bedroom. I followed him, but by the time I got there he was already cutting himself. He wasn't even shouting. Just sobbing quietly, saying how much he loved me. There was blood everywhere. The ambulance took ages to arrive. They brought us here and… I just don't want to see him again. You know he was seeing someone else? Do you think it's me? Do I attract loonies?"

I figured it was the wrong time for the truth so decided to change the subject.

"My dad's having a baby," I said.

"No fucking way."

"Next May."

"Wow." Jimmy smiled and that's when I knew he was going to be alright.

"Wow indeed," I agreed.

Mum didn't take the news as well as Jimmy. While it cheered Jimmy up and took his mind off things, it sent Mum straight for the nearest bottle. Or bottles. She spent the day drinking and then tripped over the sofa, pissed. When I tried to put her to bed, her wig fell off and she accused me of trying to scalp her. At least she didn't break anything. I spent the rest of the night worrying that she was going to throw up in her sleep and choke on her own vomit like Bon Scott did. So I got up and went back in her room to turn her onto her side.

She survived, and seemed fine next morning, calling Dad every name in the book and Doris a man-stealing slag.

So things were pretty much back to normal.

Three

Girls, Shopping Trolleys and Legless

"Hi, Billy. What're you doing?"

I was twelve and Michelle White was the true love of my life. I knew that one day we would get married, have kids and live happily ever after. It was just a matter of time.

And working up the courage to say something to her.

"Nothing," I mumbled, focusing on the work at hand.

My young internal voice let out a scream and started to call me lots of rude names. My palms were sweaty and my stomach seemed to have vanished. It dawned on me, not for the first time, that Michelle was very, very pretty.

"Don't look like nothing," Michelle giggled. "Looks like you're makin' a snowman. Aren't you a bit old for makin' snowmen?"

"It's not just any old snowman," I said, looking up from its face, where I'd been in the process of spraying tomato sauce around the mouth. "It's a zombie snowman, come back from the dead to eat people."

"Cool. Wanna play?" she asked, a coy smile appearing on her angelic face.

I did. I really wanted to play. I also wanted to say something cool and kiss her. I was twelve and couldn't help thinking it was about time I started kissing girls. After all, I didn't want to be left on the shelf.

"I am making a snowman," I replied, trying to sound as grown-up as possible but only feeling totally and utterly terrified.

"Thought you said it was a zombie," she mocked.

I managed to go even redder.

A snowball smacked into the side of my face.

I could play with her for a little while, I thought.

Another snowball flew past.

"I could've hit you if I wanted to," she laughed. "I could've…"

My aim was true. The snowball, perfectly crafted in secret from the left hand of my snowman, whacked her straight in the face.

I laughed, enjoying the taste of victory.

Michelle's lower lip started to tremble and for one terrible moment, I thought she was going to cry.

"I'm sorry. I didn't mean to hurt you. Are you okay? I'm really, really sorry."

Michelle looked up at me, her lip still trembling. My heart sank. I'd blown it with her. My one chance of true love gone. I'd die old and alone because I'd thrown a snowball at the woman I loved.

Michelle pushed me. I staggered back, straight into the snowman.

"You are so easy to fool," she laughed, pelting me with handfuls of snow as I tried and failed to get to my feet.

Eventually it dawned on me to try and throw some snowballs back.

"You will pay for that," I promised.

"Yeah, right," Michelle mocked, hurling yet more snow at me. "You're the one who's going to pay – and you're going to pay big time!"

We spent pretty much the whole day playing together.

It was a good day.

One of the best.

"Hi, Billy, what're you doing?"

Fourteen years later and not much had changed. The same killer smile, the same inability to think in her presence and the same sweaty palms. The only difference was the zombie. It was now a shopping trolley rather than a snowman.

"Nothin'," I replied, trying to ignore John's laughter.

We were in the car park of the local supermarket.

"Looks bloody stupid to me," Geoff, who was Michelle's boyfriend, remarked.

"There's nothing stupid about our little production," John snapped, moving to my side.

"It's a film we're making," I explained to Michelle, staring at my feet and trying to ignore the raw liver hanging from my shirt – not to mention the congealing cow blood covering my face.

"A film?" she answered, far more impressed than she should've been. "That's so cool."

Geoff glanced at his watch.

"Yeah, it's a mock documentary about the plight of shopping trolleys in the modern world. This is the bit where they come to life and start to eat people."

My internal voice started to scream. I sounded like the nerd from hell.

"You should do something like that," she told Geoff. "You know, something creative."

The others in our small group of film-makers had joined us. Chief among them was Kate – the real boss of the group and a cute Irish ex-punk who'd already refused to sleep with me twice on the grounds that she was happily married. She did look good though and I was well pleased when she moved next to me. I could see Michelle trying to work things out.

"Hi," she smiled. "Do you mind if I steal William for a while, only we've not got much light left and I really want to finish filming today."

Kate looped one of her arms in mine and led me away from a thoughtful Michelle. In the strange little world I lived in, it was obvious she was jealous and trying like mad to work out if anything was going on between us.

"Ready, Barry?" Kate asked our soundman.

Barry was, as usual, standing quietly in the shadows whispering to himself. At the start of the shoot, Barry had been a sweet, outspoken bloke. Then his wife had left him for a plumber and taken everything with her – including the carpet and the kids. Since then, Barry had become a little withdrawn from reality and developed a nervous and slightly scary facial tic. As he hardly ever said a word, though, he was the perfect soundman and seemed to enjoy standing around holding the microphone aloft for hours on end.

John was the final member of our crew, all part of a film-making course at the local college. He gave the camera a final check and nodded an okay. He'd joined on the pretence of, to quote: "Learning how to use one of those bastard video cameras!" but had developed a flare for lighting and design second to none. It was also a flare I was sworn to secrecy about. We were filming my death scene outside the local supermarket, as I was about to be crushed to death by the previously mentioned man-eating shopping trolleys. I was more than a little relieved to see Geoff trying to drag Michelle away from the filming. Better still, they seemed to have words and Geoff climbed into his car alone, Michelle waiting outside to see me at work.

"Positions!" Kate shouted.

A small crowd of onlookers had joined Michelle. I felt myself start to go bright red as I lay on the floor.

"Action!" Kate ordered.

On cue she started to roll the shopping trolleys towards me. They'd already been coated in raw liver and blood. I glanced up, just in time to see Michelle follow Geoff into the car. He pecked her on the head and tried to kiss her.

"No, not the trolleys," I cried out.

"Give it a bit more feeling, Billy," Kate urged.

Michelle started to kiss Geoff back.

"No, anything but that!" I screamed.

It wasn't a good day.

After we'd finished filming, I was walking home singing a song of Jimmy's to myself when I caught sight of his dad hobbling towards the Bell. That in itself wasn't unusual. Jimmy's dad was a well-known pisshead and put Mad Tommy to shame with his alcoholic intake. No, the odd thing was that he seemed to have lost one of his legs. He'd first lost it while he was in the army in Korea. Not in action but while inebriated. He was drunk and fell off a cliff. Least that's what he told me once. Jimmy and his mum worried about him pretty much all the time. He already looked like he'd had a few and was hopping along, using a brush in place of his crutch.

"Alright, Mr. Bolin. Heading for a quick one?" I said, panting by the time I caught up with him. For a one-legged drunk, Jimmy's dad could really move.

"Damn right," he said, not slowing his pace. "Doctor says I've got to give it up. Says I'm fuckin' up my liver. Bollocks to them, that's what I say."

"Don't take this the wrong way," I panted, trying to catch my breath. "But you seem to have lost your leg again."

Last time he got loose, Jimmy and me had had to search eight pubs before we found the false leg in the gents at the Black Bull.

"Wife hid it, didn't she?" he cursed, hopping closer to me. "Her and that son of mine are in it together. Trying to stop me from enjoying myself, they are. See, they reckon if they hide my leg I won't be able to get out. But I showed her. Hid my crutch as well but I've got this brush. Good it is. Not as good as a crutch, mind, but good enough to get to the pub. Feel like a pint?"

"Yeah, sure," I lied, walking with him to the pub and then phoning Jimmy and his mum to let them know he was okay.

"Alright, Billy," a voice said from the corner of the pub. I turned to see Lee sat on his own drinking a Guinness.

"Sure. You okay?" I asked.

"Yeah, fine," he lied.

I knew he was lying. He always drank in the Hope. Not only because his mum owned it, but because that was where Chrissie worked.

"We were fuckin' unlucky in that last game," he said, staring at his pint.

"We lost thirteen-one."

"Yeah, but still…" he mumbled, and then started to talk about his car. I glanced over at Jimmy's dad, who I'd left on a stool by the bar with a pint. The pint was already all but empty. Lee was a pretty good mechanic by all accounts – although it meant nothing to me. I'd never learned to drive and the last car I'd owned was by Matchbox. I think my total disinterest was a direct result of getting run over when I was six months old. My mum was crossing a road at a set of traffic lights when some bastard decided to run the red – going straight into both of us. While my pram had been totalled, we were both fine. I got lucky and landed on my head, but since then I'd always found cars a bit crap.

"So what do you think?" Lee asked.

"Bollocks to you all!" Jimmy's dad yelled from the bar.

I glanced up and noticed a few things all at the same time. The first was that he'd managed to get amazingly pissed in record time. The second was that the bloke behind the bar had decided he'd had enough and the third was that Jimmy's dad had forgotten he only had one leg and was trying to stand up without his brush. The poor sod fell backwards and collapsed onto a table where a couple were trying to have a quiet drink. It took me a second to realise the couple were Jez and his girlfriend, Becky. For all his faults, Jez had good taste in women. Becky had just moved into the house a few doors down from mine and seemed way too nice for Jez. Jimmy's dad had knocked over their table, spilling the drinks over both of them. Becky was handling it better than Jez.

"Sorry about that," I said to her, helping Mr. Bolin to his feet. Well, to his foot anyway.

"Get that fucking cripple out of here," Jez yelled, putting the table up and wiping beer off himself.

I handed Becky a cloth from the bar, trying my best to ignore Jez.

"Thanks," she smiled, catching my eyes and then looking quickly away.

"Hey, Cade – are you listening to me?" Jez said, stepping closer to me.

"Looks like you've pissed yourself," I pointed out.

Becky was trying hard not to laugh and helping Jimmy's dad stay upright.

"You're lovely, you are," Mr. Bolin slurred, swaying dangerously. "Isn't she lovely, kid?"

"Yeah," I mumbled, grateful for Lee's sudden appearance by my side, looking every inch the psycho he can be in the wrong circumstances.

"Problem, Billy?" he asked, flashing Jez one of his most dangerous smiles.

Just to add to the ambience, Jimmy and his mum rushed

in. Mrs. Bolin had obviously been panicking, while Jimmy was carrying his dad's crutch and had a look of grim acceptance on his face.

"Oh look, it's the faggot brigade," Jez snapped.

Becky was the first to react, spinning around and slapping him hard on the face.

"You are such a fucking loser," she said. "I don't know what I ever saw in you."

Jez actually raised his hand as though he was going to try and slap her back before looking around at the people watching him.

"I think you should leave now," I said.

He turned and stormed out of the pub.

"Sorry about that," Becky said, looking a little embarrassed. "He's in a… well, we've just split up so he's not in the best of moods. He's not usually like that."

Jimmy shot me a look that told me not to say a word. "You okay?" he asked her.

"Yeah, it was my idea," she said, giving me a quick smile before accepting a towel from the barmaid.

"Don't even think about it," Jimmy whispered to me. "She's a new friend and has been through enough without you screwing things up for her."

I tried and failed to look innocent.

Jimmy shook his head and turned his attention to his father. "Come on, it's time to go home."

I offered the crutch to his dad, who just stared at it, confused.

"You need a hand?" I asked.

"No, but I could do with a bloody leg," he slurred back.

Jimmy just smiled.

"I'll be fine. I'm used to this. Plus, it stops me moping. You coming to the gig later?"

"Sure. I'll see you there."

"But the pub's still open," Jimmy's dad said, on the verge of tears.

"It's later than you think," Jimmy lied. "They've just had last orders."

"What, already? Jesus, I don't know what the world's coming to."

"I'll head off with them," Becky smiled. "Thanks for... well, I'll see you around."

"Sure," I answered.

As she left, the lecherous part of my brain admired the way her bum moved in her tight black jeans.

"Your mate's not bad for an arse bandit," Lee said from behind me. "Only rear gardener I knew was in the army. Told me once that there was a club you could go in London where a dwarf would stick his head up your arse. When I told him that just wasn't possible he said you could get two fists up. Made me feel quite sick it did. He got kicked out shortly after that for shagging the CO. Think he's working at the BBC now."

"Really?" I replied, turning to face Lee, and more than a little taken aback by his knowledge of the London gay scene.

"So anyway, what should I do about Chrissie?" he asked as we went back to our table.

"How do you feel about her?" I asked, still trying to work out just what he wanted my advice on.

"Well, I fuckin' love her, don't I?" he snapped, angry that I'd conned him into using the L-word when he was still vaguely sober.

"Well, there you are then, you've answered your own question," I replied, hoping that he wouldn't notice that I'd totally missed what the question was in the first place.

"No, I've not. I asked if you thought I should…" he slowed down for a moment and placed his pint on the table. "I see what you're getting at," he nodded solemnly. "And you're right. I'm going to fuckin' marry her."

"Congratulations," I toasted.

"Definitely," he replied. "Now let's get fuckin' pissed."

And that's how I nearly lost my foreskin.

Four

Foreskins, Pain and Strange Meetings

We carried on drinking all afternoon and, before I knew it, night had arrived and I had to make it to the Rifleman's to see Dazed play. That was the name of Jimmy's band. Lee had gone back to the Hope to talk to Chrissie and quite possibly propose. I wandered into the pub alone, not really minding the fact that I was there on my own. I knew Jimmy would be somewhere around and we'd have time for a chat before he hit the stage. The kids there made me feel old. I was only twenty-six but most of the crowd looked like they should have been at home doing their homework. Quite a few were staggering around, swearing and drinking cider, convinced it made them look all grown-up.

Well, if you can't beat them, join them, I thought, buying a pint of cider from the bar before searching out Jimmy. To my surprise, he had a new skinhead in tow. He seemed a reasonable guy as well and not the least bit psychotic.

"You wanna know how to earn good money…?" he asked me

a few minutes after being introduced. "Test drugs in a clinic," he confided. "I tested some stuff the other weekend. Got three hundred quid for a couple of days' work. Piece of piss. They give you all these pills. Some are just placebos but some are fucking top. Then they monitor the effects. They didn't tell us who had what, but three of us spent all night totally wired, playing pool at a hundred miles an hour. Don't know what the fuck it was, but I wish I could get some more. Better than speed it was."

I just smiled. A weirdo drug addict was new territory for Jimmy.

"And there's no side-effects," the new guy explained, moving so close that I could smell his bad breath.

He leaned back and stared blankly to the side before moving closer again.

"And there's no side-effects," he repeated as if for the first time. "I gotta have a piss. See you in a minute."

Jimmy glanced at me expectantly, waiting for the sarcastic comment as his new friend lurched towards the gents.

"I'm on the rebound," he explained.

"What happened to Phil?" I asked, staring absent-mindedly at a woman walking by.

"He's decided to move back with his parents," Jimmy said. "Mind if we talk about something else? How about your dad?"

"I'm trying not to think about that on the grounds that it's fucking too weird. Mind if we talk about something else?"

"We're running out of topics here."

"I split up with Pam."

Jimmy raised an eyebrow.

"Okay, so technically she split up with me, but only just.

Anyway, I've decided to turn over a new leaf. No more casual sex or relationships with people I don't like."

Jimmy raised his eyebrow again.

"I'm serious."

"I'm having the strangest case of déjà vu," he smiled. "It's like we've had this conversation before. Oh, hold on. It's because we have. Every time you convince some poor girl to finish with you. Or worse still, just wander away without saying a word…"

"I'm not that shallow," I flinched.

"Cara?" Jimmy said.

"That was a one-off," I replied, sounding increasingly defensive. "And it was the FA Cup Final."

"The last words you said were…"

"…'I'm just going for a pint of milk.' I know it was wrong, but it wasn't my fault. I only popped into the Hope to tell John I wouldn't be able to watch the final with him, but one thing just led to another. It wasn't serious anyway."

"You went out with her for two months. Unless you've been keeping secrets from me, that's a personal best."

"I didn't realise Becky was so good-looking," I said.

"Yes, she's lovely. She's also been through hell, so do me a favour and stay clear of her. Anyway, aren't you still obsessed with Michelle?"

"I have no idea what you mean," I lied, much to Jimmy's amusement.

"You've not seen my acid, have you, mate?" the new boyfriend interrupted.

"I got to go," Jimmy said. "It's almost time for the set. You two have fun."

"Jimmy…" I shouted, not wanting to be left alone with his latest nutter.

"Found it," the skinhead said. "I must've dropped it."

He thought hard about this for a while and then started to laugh.

"And I'm about to drop it again," he said, placing a small bit of paper on his tongue.

I left Jimmy's boyfriend to it and went to get another cider before heading towards the stage for Dazed's set. A girl with an innocent face smiled at me and I smiled back, faintly recognising her from somewhere I couldn't remember. Everyone apart from me seemed to be in groups, laughing and joking.

Another pint vanished. It had been a long day.

A few chords hit out as Jimmy started the gig. Dazed was a cool four-piece but it was Jimmy's band. He was lead guitarist, vocalist and songwriter. I started to sing along to "No One Loves No One", one of his best songs.

"He's great isn't he?" the girl said as he finished his second encore.

"Yeah, he is," I replied, turning away from her.

She kept on talking and we both kept on drinking and before long it was gone midnight and I was with the girl who was seventeen and we were in the fields behind the pub and I was again having sex with someone I couldn't give a fuck about.

I tried to work out just exactly what I was doing and why, when she whispered that it was her first time. We carried on and as I finished I felt a searing pain down below.

Almost as soon as it was over, she smiled and staggered back to the pub and a gaggle of waiting mates, who all started laughing and cheering as soon as she joined them. Left on my own, I became aware that my dick was still throbbing. I went to pull my trousers up and froze with horror as I saw blood dripping from the edge of my now limp prick. The foreskin had split open and the poor thing was starting to swell and not looking very well at all.

"It's God," I mumbled to myself. "He's punishing me for breaking my vow. I'm sorry, God. Please let it be okay. Please. I'll start to believe in you again and go to church every Sunday and everything. Honest. Just don't kill my dick."

"Did you have a nice night, dear?" my mum asked as I crept into the house, so scared I'd not even got a kebab.

"Yeah," I lied, staggering upstairs and collapsing on my bed. Tears were in my eyes as I removed my trousers and dared to look down at myself. There was blood all over the end. I turned off the light and went to bed.

"It'll be fine in the morning. It'll be fine in the morning. It'll be fine in the morning," I whimpered again and again, before drifting off into a nightmarish sleep filled with blood and screaming virgins.

It wasn't better in the morning. It was worse. A *lot* worse. It had swollen badly and was throbbing like crazy. I knew for sure I was going to die.

I ran a bath, hoping the water would help ease the pain, and screamed when the cut made contact with the water.

I decided to never have a bath again.

It looked weird and misshapen. I thought about going to the

doctor but couldn't get through to the surgery.

By noon I was in a blind panic and banging on Jimmy's door. He opened it wearing only a towel and looking a little the worse for wear. I ignored his condition and barged straight in.

"I'm dying," I said.

"Really? Tell you what, I'll put some clothes on. You make us both a cup of coffee and then you can tell me about it."

"You don't understand. It's my, well… it's… it's not got long left. It might be dead by the time you get dressed."

Jimmy offered me a bemused, questioning smile and left for his bedroom. Annoyed that he didn't seem to be taking my impending death with the seriousness it deserved, I put the kettle on.

By the time he'd returned, I'd drunk most of my coffee while pacing his living room trying not to think about my damaged member.

"Okay," he asked. "What's wrong?"

I gave him a recap of the previous night's events.

"You're not going to die," he smirked. "Sounds like you've just split your foreskin. Happened to me once, though I'll spare you the sordid details. It's painful but not the end of the world. Give it a couple of days and everything will be back to normal."

"You sure?"

"Yeah. A week, tops. It serves you right for taking advantage of that poor, innocent girl."

"I wasn't taking advantage of her, she almost forced me, and how do you know about that anyway?"

"I have my sources," Jimmy replied. "You know, this reminds me of that time when we were kids and my mum thought boys should be circumcised. Do you remember?"

I pretended not to.

"We were both about twelve. I think she'd read some article in a magazine about it. Anyway, we both heard her talking about it and you ran screaming into the back garden and refused to come in until they promised no one was going to touch you."

"Can you blame me? Would you want someone coming near your dick with a scalpel?"

"That's not the point. The point is you always dramatise things."

"Jimmy, you out there?" a voice shouted from the bedroom.

It sounded like the weirdo drug addict from the night before.

"Don't worry, it'll heal up by the weekend," he said, leading me out of the house.

I left, sulking at my friend's indifference but also relieved that my dick wasn't going to die.

Maybe it's time to stop drinking, I thought, crossing the road back to my house. I was just opening the front gate when someone tapped me on the shoulder.

"I thought it was you," Michelle said.

I tried to look cool and attractive, but judging by the smile on her face failed on all counts.

My palms were sweaty and I suddenly remembered dancing with her when I was eight in Mrs Kilgannon's country dance-class, and how nice her hand felt in mine.

"How's things?" she asked, after a few seconds of awkward silence.

Not very good, I thought. *I've got an Elastoplast on the end of my dick.*

"Fine," I lied.

We fell silent for a few eternities and stared at the pavement and trees and walls.

"How are you?" I asked, trying to break the silence.

"Fine, thanks," she replied, pausing for a moment before adding, "Did you hear I split with Geoff?"

"Really?" I answered, trying not to grin. "When?"

"Last night. Found out he was seeing someone else. I told him to make a choice and he did."

"I'm sorry."

"Don't be. I'm better off without him."

"That's true," I said, making Michelle laugh.

"You don't like him much, do you?" She smiled.

I just shook my head.

"I don't know why, but he's not fond of you at all either. Was that Cassie I saw you with last night?"

"Cassie?"

"At the gig?"

"Oh, her. No, at least I don't think so. I wasn't with her anyway. We were just chatting."

"Oh. So you're not seeing anyone at the moment?"

"Nah, I like the single life too much."

What!? Did I really just say that? My mind cursed. *Idiot!!*

"Oh. So you're not seeing anyone?" she repeated.

"No."

"Have you ever been to the Raven since they've done it up?"

She seemed a little strange, as if she was waiting for me to say something.

A thought hit me as lightning threatened to strike.

"Do you want to go there sometime, maybe for a drink or something?" I coughed, trying not to make it sound too serious. It was a stupid thing to say. There was no way she'd want to go out with me. There was just no way she'd…

"Yes, I'd love to, when?"

want to

go out

with…

Hold it. What did she just say?

"I said, I'd love to go there. How about tonight?"

"Tonight's great," I replied instinctively.

A pain in my nether regions reminded me that later that day probably wasn't the best of ideas.

"No, sorry," I added quickly. "I've got something on tonight."

Like lying curled up in my bed sobbing quietly until the pain goes away…

My mind started racing. It was Saturday and Jimmy had said it needed a few days to heal and I got paid by John on Thursday but Thursday was a crap day to go out with someone…

"How about Friday?" I suggested.

"Yeah, Friday's fine. About eight?"

"Cool. I'll see you there."

"Okay."

I stood there for a while and watched Michelle walk back to her house. I looked up to the sky and I swear the sun came out from behind some clouds.

I stayed there grinning for a while.

"Bloody hell," I managed to mumble, before going into my house to tell Happy the good news.

Five

Starkers, Haircuts and Old Friends

Lee hadn't asked Chrissie to marry him. He'd bottled it at the last minute. He told me this down the Hope when he was trying to drink himself into a coma as punishment.

"I love her," he slurred, as I poured him another pint. "So why didn't I ask her?"

"I don't know. Maybe you have a problem expressing yourself." "I do not!" he snapped. "Only last night I told her I fancied the fuck out of her."

"That's not sharing emotions, Lee. That's trying to get a shag. There's a difference."

"Billy, can I have a word?" John asked, casting a despairing look at his brother. "On a scale of one to ten, how drunk do you think our kid is?"

"He's had a few," I answered.

"That's what I was worried about. Do you think he can see

straight?"

Right on cue, Lee slid off his barstool and decided to lie face down on the floor for a while.

"Bollocks," John cursed.

"He'll be okay," I said. "Maybe you can just take him upstairs. Let him sleep it off for a while."

"Fuck him," John said. "Let the bastard stay where he is."

"John, he's your brother…"

"And part of the pool team," John explained. "See that bunch of wankers over there?"

I followed his gaze to five too-cool-by-half blokes playing pool.

"They're from the Greyhound. The pool tournament starts in ten minutes and guess who our key player is?"

I flinched as I looked towards Lee, who was dragging himself back on to his barstool and asking a coat I'd hung behind the bar for a pint.

"He can't play pool like that," I said, not seeing the penny as it dropped right past me.

"Exactly. That's where you come in."

"But I'm crap at pool."

"You're just being modest. You tried out for the team. You were good an' all. Besides, we're desperate – you're the only sober one in the pub."

I glanced around the bar and realised he was right. As I'd been working, I hadn't had a drop to drink all night.

"Okay," I said. "Seeing as it's an emergency."

"Good. Let's go to the toilet."

"Sorry, John. I'll play pool with you but I refuse to have your babies."

"You taking the piss?"

A flash of John's psycho side popped out, making me shake my head frantically, my voice a few octaves higher the next time I spoke.

"No, it was just a joke, that's all. Why do you want me to go into the toilet with you, though? Shouldn't I have a practice or something?"

"It's a team talk. We've got a trick up our sleeves," he laughed.

A little nervous, I followed John into the toilets and found myself confronted by three fat, middle-aged men. Three fat, *naked*, middle-aged men.

"Okay," John ordered, pulling off his jeans. "Get your kit off."

"What?" I said, trying not to look at any of the naked male flesh around me.

"Get your kit off. We're going to play them stark bollock naked. Should put the shits up them."

"I can't play pool naked."

"Why not?" John asked, removing his underpants.

"Because I can't. That's why. It's just not done. People are watching."

"If we win, we get a hundred quid each."

"It's not about money," I declared.

"Go on, lad. Get your kecks off," one of the fat blokes said. "What's the matter, you some kind of puff?"

"I'm sorry, but I can't play pool naked. It's against my religion. And it'd put me right off. In fact, I'm already starting to feel a little queasy."

"Okay, have it your way," John conceded. "I guess four of us naked should do the trick. I'm disappointed though. I thought you were more of a man."

"I'd rather you remain disappointed than the alternative," I said, following them out of the toilet to the cries that awaited us.

"Sometimes this pub really scares me," I mumbled.

Despite my clothing, the plan nearly worked. After an initial argument that playing pool naked was illegal – an argument silenced by a smile from John – the games started and the Greyhound seemed more than a tad distracted. They were clearly intimidated by our genitals and seemed disinclined to touch the table after we'd played our balls (so to speak). The match was halfway through when things started to go wrong, as Pat started to scratch his nether regions a bit more than strictly necessary.

"Pat, do you mind? You're just supposed to put the opposition off, not your team-mates," I said, taking the cue from him for my shot.

"Sorry," he apologised. "My crabs are playing up again."

I missed a couple of sitters after that, not really wanting to use the same cue as Pat. The Greyhound made a comeback.

Sod's law meant the last match was mine. Pat had retired injured after John hit him with a cue. It didn't bother me, though. I'd regained my stride and, after initial nervousness, had decided to make the best of it. After all, I wasn't naked and we were still winning. By the last game, I was feeling pretty cocky. The first few balls went down with ease. People started to cheer as I made some truly remarkable shots. This was my game. Despite my lack of nudity, I was the star of the team. People would talk about this game for years, and not just because of the naked Northern blokes. I was on the black and grinning when Life decided to clobber me with a baseball bat. He did so by getting Lee to grab me by the shoulders to let me in on a secret he'd already told me three times that night.

"I'm going to do it," he said. "I'm going to ask her."

"Good. About bloody time," I said, smiling at Chrissie.

John had asked her to come in and cover for me so I could play pool. She smiled and rolled her eyes.

"Chrissie!" he yelled loudly, getting everyone's attention.

Chrissie covered her eyes with a hand but seemed amused by the whole thing.

"I fuckin' love you," Lee yelled. "Will you marry me?"

"Course I will, you daft bugger," Chrissie answered.

"You've just made me the happiest man in the whole pub," Lee grinned, then passed out on the pool table, scattering my balls all over the place.

In the rematch I got beat good and proper. Their guy cleaned up and I didn't even make it to the table. Lee was not popular with his brother and it suddenly dawned on me I really should know better than to play pool with a bunch of naked Northern blokes.

What's this Life and the baseball bat theory?

Okay, first off, it's only partially my theory. It sort of developed between myself and a pal called Bill a few years ago and goes like this. There are times in your life when everything's going well and all's cool. When this happens, you're climbing a metaphysical cliff face, trying to reach the top, where you've heard the view is amazing. Each time you say something like, "Life's turned around for me", or the classic "I'm in love and this is going to work", you're climbing higher and higher.

At one point, you actually reach the summit and the view really is as good as you've heard. It's so good you relax and think: "That's it. I've made it. Everything's going to work out now," and that's the moment Life takes you out. You see, Life is actually a seven-foot clown in bad make-up carrying a baseball bat. On the side of the baseball bat is a single word.

Reality.

He smacks you with the bat and sends you all the way to the bottom of the cliff, where you remain for a while, confused, trying to work out what happened and how everything went so horribly wrong so quickly.

Of course, Life doesn't only smack you in big ways. It also does so in really small, irritating ways. Like making you miss buses and trains and job interviews or making some drunk ruin your chances of winning the pool tournament by falling onto the table at a crucial moment in the proceedings.

Sometime later I was outside my front door trying to eat the last bit of my kebab and turn the key in the lock at the same time. And women say men can't multitask. As I ended up dropping the kebab meat on the floor, they might have a point. I was looking down at it, trying to work out whether it would still be edible, when I heard shouting from across the road. I turned just in time to see Jez getting slapped by Becky. She seemed furious about something and ran inside her flat. Jez tried to follow, only to have the door slammed in his face. He stayed outside for a while, shouting her name and even saying "Please!" at one point, before turning and seeing me.

"Evening," I smiled, enjoying the show.

He didn't say a word as he climbed in his car and drove off.

Friday came quicker than expected and started well. I was calm, relaxed and feeling cool.

That should have warned me.

About noon I ventured out to get a paper and passed the local barber's. A thought hit me. I needed a haircut. A quick glance in the shop window told me that my hair was at best ill-kept and at worst like something a mental patient might have had circa nineteen-seventy-seven. Now Aunt Jean usually came down to cut my hair but she was in Tunisia for two weeks with her toy boy. I didn't need that much doing, though, so figured the local barber would be safe enough. His name was Fred and he was one of those old-school barbers who operate out of the small shacks that mysteriously appeared in the middle of every major city and town around nineteen-fifty-three and have remained the same ever since. "What can I do you for?" he joked in a London accent.

My grandma, just after she went senile, warned me never to trust Londoners.

"Just need a trim," I explained, moving towards the empty chair.

"What you need, my son, is a short back and sides. You'd look right smart with a short back and sides."

"I kind of like it the way it is. Just need a bit off the top and the back tidying up."

"Fair enough, son. Fair enough. Shouldn't take long. What about the weather, ain't it awful?"

I wasn't really in the mood for small talk so just nodded and smiled in the right places, which he didn't seem to mind. The whole thing only took five minutes.

I'd always thought murder took longer.

"How's that, then?" he declared.

Now here's the thing, have you noticed that when you're sitting in a hairdresser's and you look in the mirror, your hair always looks longer than it really is?

It happens to me all the time, so that was why I looked at my reflection and said:

"Could you take a little more off the top?"

Somewhere a bell started to toll.

Half an hour later found me knocking on Jimmy's door, wanting to talk about my forthcoming date.

"Billy, something wrong?" he asked, as he opened the door.

He looked at my hair straight away.

It must be good, I thought, *he looks amazed!*

"Just calling for a chat," I said.

"See you've had a haircut," he smiled, as I followed him into the kitchen.

"Yeah, what do you think?"

He looked straight at my hair and caught my eyes before looking away nervously.

"Tell me something, did you go to one of those places in town?"

"Not exactly."

"Didn't think so. Did you, by any chance, go to that little shack up the road?"

"Might've done," I answered, starting to feel a little nervous.

He ran his hand through the top of my hair.

"I suppose if you have the front spiked… No, that doesn't work."

He fell silent for a moment and looked a little uneasy.

"You don't like it, do you?" I stuttered, as an awful realisation started to sink in.

"Maybe it's just me…"

"What don't you like about it?"

He motioned me to a mirror hanging over his gas fire.

"Okay, take a look."

I did – and started to panic.

I had P.H.T. *Post Haircut Trauma*. I'd asked the old bastard to cut it short at the top and pretty much leave the back alone. He'd done just that. The back still looked as stupid as it had earlier – only now looked even worse because the top was so short. I opened my mouth, but no words came out. There were inbred hicks in the Deep South of the United States who possessed better haircuts.

"It's not that bad," Jimmy lied.

I let out a sad, plaintive whine.

"No, really. It's…" Jimmy paused for a moment. "Isn't it tonight you're going out with Michelle?"

I nodded slowly, feeling like a condemned man.

"Houston, I think we have a problem," Jimmy said, trying to make light of the situation.

"A problem," I whimpered. "I've got more than a problem. He's killed my hair."

"He hasn't killed it," Jimmy said, passing me a mug of tea. "He's just hurt it. A lot."

"He's fucking killed it. And he's ruined my life. The bastard. Probably did it on purpose. There's no way I can see Michelle like this. Why did I get a haircut anyway? It looked all right this morning."

"No it didn't," Jimmy reminded me. "Your hair looked awful. You really should take more care of yourself. Hair's important."

"Yeah, okay, okay. But what am I going to do? I've only got a few hours before I meet her and if I go like this, she'll think I'm retarded."

"Well, you are retarded."

"Thanks a lot."

"Sorry."

Jimmy fell silent for a moment, and seemed to be carefully considering something.

"Christ, I need a drink," I whispered.

"No, you need a haircut. A good one." He bit his lower lip and looked worried.

"You okay?" I asked, not used to seeing Jimmy look so serious.

"Sure," he half laughed. "Just let me make a couple of calls. I know someone who can help."

"Really?"

"I don't know. It's been a few years since…" Jimmy's voice trailed off. "I'll see what I can do."

He picked up his mobile and dialled a few numbers. Trying to track down an old friend called Gabriel. I'd never heard the name before, but that didn't surprise me. While I always poured out my heart to Jimmy, he didn't always tell me the details of his own life.

"Yeah, I know, but this is kind of important," Jimmy said.

He half smiled at me but seemed to be trying to keep something in check.

"I know. But that was a long time ago, you know. Things change." His voice went a little lower and I couldn't make out the rest.

"Hey, it's okay," I started to say. "I'm sure I can find somewhere to save it."

Jimmy waved me silent with an arm and carried on talking.

"No. He's not *that* sort of friend. It's Billy, you remember me telling you about him? That's right. That was him. Well, anyway, he's just had a haircut this morning. A bad haircut, and he's got an important date tonight. You remember Michelle? Well he eventually got around to asking her out. Yeah, I know. So can you fit him in?"

There was another moment's silence. As though whoever was on the other end of the phone was giving some serious thought to their answer.

"You can? Great. I'll send him over. No, I can't, I'm afraid. Got a few things to do. Yeah, maybe some other time. See you."

Jimmy put down the phone and seemed miles away for a while. A brief smile crossed his face and then he was back to normal.

"Right, that's fixed," he said. "You've got an appointment at four o'clock at a place called Heaven. It's run by Gabriel, an old friend of mine – if he can't save your hair, nobody can."

"Thanks," I smiled. "I owe you one."

"Don't worry about it," Jimmy said. "Who knows, tonight you might meet the love of your life. Course, if that turns out to be Michelle, you have my deepest sympathy."

A lot of things about James' recent life choices started to make sense when I met Gabriel. He was a vicious-looking skinhead in Doc Marten boots and a tight T-shirt. About six-two, with Celtic tattoos on each muscular arm.

"Not what you expected, am I?" he grinned, enjoying my confusion. "Guess James never showed you any photos."

He sounded a little nervous.

"James was right, that really is a mess," he said, looking at my hair. "I don't think even I can save that. Maybe if I shaved it all off?"

The blood rushed to my face and Gabriel burst out laughing. "Relax, I'm joking. It'll be fine."

I was still too nervous to relax. There were mirrors all over the place. Each one reflected my appalling hair from a different angle.

"It won't be a problem. You'll have to have it quite short, though. You went to Fred, didn't you?"

I nodded, miles away. I was busy trying to think back to the time Gabriel would have known Jimmy. It had to be around the time I tried college. Which was also around the time Jimmy's fixation with skinheads began. Things were starting to fall into place.

"We get a few people here after seeing him. He's good at the old short back and sides but bugger-all use for anything else. Especially since he got back from the war."

I was led to one of the chairs and covered in a smock. Gabriel sprayed my hair with water, combed it and started to cut. He talked about a lot of things but seemed to be skirting around something important.

"By the way," he eventually said, trying to sound casual. "How's James? I've not seen him in four or five years."

"He's fine. Did you used to…"

"A long time ago. Didn't work out."

"Sorry."

"No need to be. These things happen. There we are. Good as new."

I looked in the mirror and grinned. Somehow he'd saved it.

"That's perfect," I said. "How much do I owe you?"

"Nothing. You're a friend of James. It's on the house."

"Cheers."

"Hope it all works out tonight."

"It'd make a change," I smiled, pushing the door open to leave the shop.

"Oh," Gabriel added, trying to make his words sound like an afterthought. "Remember to tell James I was asking after him."

Six

Date Night, Thieves and the End of the World

Before I knew what was happening it was already eight thirty and I was outside the Raven feeling more than a little nervous. A little bit of me had been in love with Michelle since I was eight, when her family had moved into the house opposite. I used to hide behind the dustbins when I saw her, too scared to talk.

So what's changed? I asked myself, only too aware of my sweaty palms and beating heart.

It's just a date, I reminded myself. *Nothing special.*

It had been a long time since I'd been on a date with someone I actually liked. I wasn't quite sure what to do. I thought about walking around the block a few times but dismissed it as a dumb idea. It was after eight thirty and she could've already been in the pub. Plus, even if she wasn't, I needed a few drinks to mellow me out before she arrived. Taking a deep breath, I stepped through the door. The place was pretty empty for a Friday night. A few people scattered here and there.

"Hi, Billy. Fancy meeting you here."

It was the girl from the gig. Down below shrivelled up, still not totally over the pain.

"Hi. You okay?" I smiled pleasantly enough.

What the fuck was her name?

"You looked a bit sick the other night," she said.

Not surprising, you nearly killed my dick.

"Yeah, guess I had a little too much to drink."

"Here on your own?"

There it was. The familiar hope in her voice. I recognised it all too well from my own sad attempts to talk to women I really liked. Guess the girl still had a crush on me. Hardly surprising, even though it hadn't been my greatest performance, it was probably good enough to make her obsessed.

Poor deluded chick.

"Just meeting a friend," I said, getting ready to let her down gently.

"You okay, Cassie?" a voice asked.

Some too-cool-for-his-own-good teenage hipster appeared out of nowhere and wrapped an arm around whatshername. She pecked him on the cheek and gave him a hug. Seconds later they were kissing in a quiet corner of the pub.

Probably on the rebound from yours truly, I thought, deciding to ignore the fact that the new boyfriend was younger, fitter and better-looking than me.

I glanced at the time and was ordering a drink when the barmaid turned and smiled at me.

Becky?

Was everyone I knew in the pub tonight? I looked around in

case Jimmy and Mum were having a coffee in the corner.

She'd changed her hair again. It was still long but now had cool-looking purple streaks at the ends.

For a second I was lost for words.

"Good to see a friendly face," she smiled. "It's my first night."

It was a good smile and for a second I couldn't remember Michelle's name.

God, I was shallow.

"Used to work in the Greyhound," Becky explained. "But Jez drinks there so I felt a little distance might do me some good."

"And it's all of a mile from the Greyhound," I smiled back.

"You know what I mean," she said. "Ice?"

She had a lovely smile.

"In your JD, do you want ice?"

"Yeah. In fact, could you make it a double?"

"Got a date?" she asked, taking a measure from the bottle.

For once I decided to tell the truth.

"Yeah, Michelle."

Sure it was my imagination, but she seemed a little taken aback by this.

"Of course, Jimmy mentioned it earlier. Good luck. You've liked her for years, haven't you?"

I flinched a little. Not really wanting to tell her how I felt for Michelle.

"Guess," I replied. I glanced around, unable to meet Becky's smile and not quite sure why I suddenly felt so confused. I turned back when I heard a smash. Becky was holding a broken glass in her hand.

"Stupid glasses," she cursed. "Caught it on the optics."

"Shit, you okay?" I asked, handing her some clean tissues.

"Fine," she replied, a little dazed.

"You should sit down for a bit," I said, noticing the glass had cut the palm of her right hand.

"No… I'll be fine. I… I need this job."

"You okay?" a deep and slightly dodgy voice said from the door to the back of the pub. A thickset, beer-bellied landlord appeared, looking pissed off.

"I'm fine," she lied.

"She needs to get that cleaned," I told him.

"He's right, love. Sheila!" he yelled.

"But… it's my first night."

"Sheila!" he yelled again. Feet thundered down the stairs and an exceptionally large and ferocious-looking woman appeared, her hair in curlers.

"What's the matter?" she shouted in a thick Irish accent.

"The new girl's gone and hurt herself. I don't think it's serious but she should get it looked at just in case. Have you got the first-aid kit?"

"Course. Let's have a look."

I winced as she grabbed Becky's hand, squeezing it so more blood started to seep out.

"Might need stitches in that. Come on love, I'll take you to A&E."

"No, honestly, I'm fine. It's just a little cut."

"You can never be too safe. Sheila's Uncle Albert cut his hand once and didn't get it seen to. Thing got all infected and he had to have it cut off, didn't he, love?"

"That's right. They cut it right off, they did. Put one of them hooks in its place."

"Yeah, but that way back," I interrupted, trying to change the line of their conversation. "They hardly ever put hooks on these days."

"It was only a few years ago," Sheila replied, giving me daggers.

"I just feel so stupid," Becky mumbled, as the landlady followed her out of the pub.

"Don't be silly. We all have accidents," I smiled. "Probably my fault for distracting you."

The owner looked at me.

"Yeah, definitely my fault, thinking about it. Sorry about that."

As they reached the door, Becky turned and whispered thanks.

"You'll be fine," I mouthed, finding myself actually worried about her.

"Stupid cow," her boss said, as soon as they'd gone. "What do you want, mate?"

"I thought she was pretty good," I said. "One of the best barmaids I've seen in a while."

"Yeah?" He seemed a little unconvinced. "I don't know. It's hard to get good staff these days. Still, she is a looker and that always helps attract the punters. So what you havin'?"

"Double Jack and Coke, thanks."

He turned to make my drink and I took a quick look at the clock. It was now eight forty-five and not quite the nice quiet start to the evening I'd planned. I took my drink and walked over to the jukebox, glancing a little nervously around the pub.

Michelle would be here soon. Maybe we'd move on somewhere. I put a few of my favourite songs on the jukebox and went to a nearby table, smiling as I caught sight of my reflection in a mirror.

My hair really did look good.

Okay, so the night hadn't started out well but it'd get better.

I could tell.

9.00.

Thirty minutes late. I checked my phone for messages. Nothing. No problem. I tried to ignore the sense of impending doom.

9.15.

Time for a few more whiskies. Just for a little extra relaxation.

Maybe there was a bus strike or something. I checked the local news on my phone. No bus strikes.

9.30.

Okay, so now she was an hour late. A few more whiskies were required. I toyed with the idea of calling her up but decided against it on the grounds it'd only make me sound desperate. So I sent her a text message instead. Far better than calling… Maybe I'd got the night wrong.

Or the pub wrong.

Or the year wrong…

9.45.

My call went straight to her voicemail. Time for another Jack. I sulked back to the table, starting to feel very uncomfortable. Other people in the pub were talking about me. I could tell. Especially Cassie. She was probably having a good laugh. And that other couple sat by the bar looking all lovey-dovey, touching and kissing and all happy and stuff.

Bastards.

10.00.

I was beginning to get the distinct impression Michelle wasn't going to show. The Jack had started to take effect and I was beginning to suspect that Life really was a complete and utter bastard.

10.15.

Fuck.

10.30.

I decided to go home and cry.

Or kill myself.

Instead I settled for a kebab.

10.45.

The night was officially fucked. The kebab was shit and I was stuck at the arse end of town.

It was all Michelle's fault.

I wonder why she didn't turn up?

Guess she didn't like me after all.

I was traipsing aimlessly through the streets, my hands greasy from the kebab. The meat was cold but that didn't stop me from shovelling it into my mouth. I needed to walk. There was no way I could go home. I needed time to myself. To try and work out why she hadn't shown. Maybe I should call her again. No. Fuck it. If she really liked me she'd have shown. Bet she was just using me to make Geoff jealous.

Fucker.

Not that I cared. He was welcome to her. I remembered him from school. He was a cunt. Used to be captain of the rugby team and hang out with Jez. Their idea of a good time was pulling the trousers off first-years and covering their balls with shoe polish.

Always hated the fuckers.

The bad egg smell coming from the glass factory hit me. Christ, I needed to get out of this shithole.

"Hey, mate… " a voice called from the shadows.

Great. It was probably a mugger.

"Billy, that you?"

I recognised the voice from the Hope.

"Charlie?"

"Yeah. Come here. Got something for you."

Pissed and a little puzzled, I went down the alley and saw Charlie sitting on an old stone wall next to a large bin bag with something metallic inside. He was smoking a spliff. A big spliff.

"Do you want some blow? It's fuckin' good stuff."

The light was bad in the alley but I could tell from his voice that he was totally stoned.

I sat next to him and took the spliff, hoping it would help me to relax.

"Thanks," I said, inhaling deeply.

"That's fucking good stuff," I coughed. "Where d'you get it?"

"Mate," he said, cryptically touching his nose.

I took a couple more long ones before giving it him back.

"So what you doin' around here?" he asked.

"Got stood up," I explained.

"Women. They're all bastards. My wife… I have one little… one little…"

He fell silent for a moment.

"Wanna hear a joke?" he asked, passing me the spliff again.

"What?"

"A joke. To cheer you up. It's never easy, love. But jokes are good so here's one. You don't need a parachute to go skydiving," Charlie said, and then drifted off for a moment before continuing, "But you do need a parachute to go skydiving twice."

I giggled a little but didn't feel that good. In fact, I was starting to feel a little edgy and weird. Normally after a couple of puffs I felt relaxed but this… I'd never really had the heebie-jeebies before.

"Fuckin' hell," I said.

"Yeah," Charlie mumbled.

He was a decent sort of bloke, Charlie.

At least he was when I was pissed and stoned.

"You're a fucking good footballer. You are," he told me, passing me a fresher, thicker spliff. I lit it and took a puff in the hope that it'd make me feel better.

"Fuckin' good," he repeated.

"We make a good team. No one can get past us," I lied.

"Yeah," he cried, rising to his feet. "No one can fucking beat us!"

His foot kicked whatever was in the bin bag and a dog started barking from the back of one of the nearby houses.

"What's in the bag?" I asked, as he lifted it up.

"New games console," he explained. "Can you hold it a sec? I really need a piss."

"Sure."

I took the bin bag off Charlie as he wandered deeper into the alley for a piss. The dog's barking seemed to be getting louder. It sounded quite vicious.

"Where did you get it?" I shouted, just able to make out Charlie leaning against the alley wall.

"One of these houses," he replied, wobbling back towards me.

"You mean you just bought it off someone?" I asked, a little nervous.

"Yeah, right," he laughed.

Oh fuck.

Right on cue, an old man came out of the back of a house with an Alsatian.

"You can have this back now," I said, virtually throwing the bin bag and its contents at him.

"Who's there?" the man yelled. "I've called the police."

Amazingly enough, Charlie caught the bag and started to walk casually away.

"Thanks for the help," he said. "I'll see you on Sunday."

A police siren started getting louder and louder.

"I'm gonna let Rebel off her lead in a second. She used to be a police dog," the man warned.

Charlie had vanished into thin air but I couldn't move. I heard the Alsatian bark and decided to run... suddenly remembering that Charlie had already been nicked once for breaking and entering.

I was not built for jail.

I didn't stop running for a very long time.

Time blurred and the world started to get very fucking weird. I stopped and leaned against a wall trying to catch my breath. The kebab was not sitting well with the Jack and pot. My nerves were shot to fuck and I couldn't breathe. Everything went black as I decided to have a little lie-down...

"The world is doomed!"

A drunken tramp was prodding me with his finger and ranting about sinners. I didn't have a clue who, what, or where I was. I staggered to my feet, balancing against the wall. My mouth tasted of sick and I looked down at my shirt to see a bit of a mess there.

"You're in a right state, mate," the drunken tramp warned me.

I was in no state to argue and started to shamble down the road, trying to work out just where I was. An old man was standing in the middle of a junction directing traffic – completely naked apart from some rabbit slippers. As I stumbled by, he smiled at a kindred spirit. A nearby sign read Honeydale Hospital and it all started to make some kind of sense. I was at the far end of town, near the mental hospital that used to be one of the biggest in the country. I didn't know how far home was but I knew the general direction and somehow managed to make it back there, blessed by whatever god watches over drunks. As I entered the street, a mist was starting to rise, although that might've just been the drink. A door slammed and I looked up to see Becky walking from Jimmy's to her own house. I raised my hand to wave. Any kind of thought and movement was proving very difficult. As I tried to work out which of the keys in my hand was the best to try in the front door (I seemed to have a lot more than usual), a car pulled up outside Michelle's. Geoff got out and ran up to the door. She answered, dressed only in a towel, and kissed him passionately. I spent a few decades looking at them kiss and started to feel completely shit. More vomit started to trickle from my mouth. An instant later, I doubled up puking. Every kebab I'd ever had came back to haunt me. When I looked over the road at the happy couple, they were both looking in my direction and laughing. I started to wobble a bit and decided to have a long lie-down.

Seven

Hangovers, Baseball Bats and Engagements

Excuse me while I vomit.

Cough cough.

Fucked…

Pleasegodinheavendon'tletmedieidon'twanttodielikethischokingonmyownvomitiwanttoliveireallydoi…

fuck…

notevenpukinganymore.

Blood… I swear that was blood!

fuckfuckfuckfuckfuckfuckfuckfuckfuck

Bed… sleep…

Can't sleep. Feel like shit. Need fresh air. That helps.

Kneeling on muddy grass in the middle of the night trying not to die. This isn't good. Isn't good at all.

The rain's hitting me… I'm going to catch pneumonia… bed…

Up the stairs… I hate stairs… they're so very hard…

Bed… sleep… doors… forgot to lock the back door…

More stairs… the dog's following me up.
He's licking the bowl of vomit.
Ugghh.
Happy's now licking my face. The smell…
Sorry Happy.
oh god.
…
…
oh god.

I was standing on a cloud outside the Pearly Gates. St. Peter wasn't happy with me. As an atheist, I couldn't help feeling this meant I was in a lot of trouble. Especially when St. Peter looked just like Charlie and offered me a spliff. Angels were singing and I wanted to go home…

I was in the road outside my house. The sky was melting. Everyone in the street was laughing and I couldn't work out why.

I woke and felt very, very ill.

Everything was a little strange as I staggered to the bathroom to get a glass of water.

"BILLY. ARE YOU OKAY NOW?"

Why was my mother shouting?

"I SAID ARE YOU OKAY NOW – AFTER ALL THAT FUSS IN THE STREET LAST NIGHT?"

"Please, Mum. I just need to sleep… and there's no need to shout."

"I'M NOT SHOUTING. IF I WAS SHOUTING I'D BE **SHOUTING LIKE THIS!**"

"Point taken… now please… jus' wanna sleep."

The dog started barking very loudly. I looked at him and

could've sworn he was doing it on purpose. I had no idea why.

"SO YOU DON'T WANT TO KNOW ABOUT US ALL COMING OUT TO PULL YOU OFF GEOFF…"

"Not really. Tell me later – when my brain stops hurting."

I made it back to bed and decided to hide there until the pain went away and my stomach stopped impersonating a lava lamp.

In the dream, Michelle was looking at me, her eyes filled with desire. Geoff tried to hit me but I blocked his punch and landed a cool one in return. It floored Geoff and Michelle ran into my arms, smothering me in kisses while the whole street looked on and applauded. Everything was good and we all lived happily ever after.

The End.

"Is he okay now?"

"See for yourself."

My mum came into my bedroom with Jimmy. I placed a pillow over my head and pretended to be asleep. It was safer that way.

"Is he alive?" Jimmy asked her.

"When he finds out what he did last night he'll wish he wasn't."

"It was embarrassing, wasn't it?"

"In front of everybody too," my mum added. "I could have died."

"Go away," I mumbled.

They didn't.

"Please?"

"I'll be in all day if he wants to pop round for a chat," Jimmy said.

"Thanks for everything," my mum said as they left the room. "Some of his so-called friends would have just left him there – especially after that little performance."

Oh god.

I tried to ignore the rest of the day but it refused to go away. About four in the afternoon I staggered downstairs and sat in front of the TV for a while. I made a point of not looking in any mirrors. Mum had gone out somewhere and the dog wouldn't come near me. My mum had made sure to leave a bowl and a sponge at the top of the stairs, close to a very clean toilet. The carpet nearby had also been scrubbed so I guess I hadn't quite made it there on one of my many trips during the night.

The dog was looking clean as well. I guess Mum must have washed him but I had no idea why.

My head still hurt.

A lot.

A while later my mum came back in and the dog rushed to meet her at the door. She dumped the shopping in the kitchen before coming into the living room to make fun of the dead.

"How are you feeling?" she asked, handing me a glass filled with aspirin.

There was just about enough life in me to mumble a reply.

"The whole street's talking about you. I'm ashamed, I really am."

She paused and I readied myself for the horrid truth. If you can't remember something, surely that means it never happened?

"So from what I can gather, you were just lying in the gutter, unconscious, when Geoff arrived at Michelle's but then you staggered over and proclaimed your love for Michelle. Everyone in the street heard you. Brenda and a few of the others came out to watch. They said you started to threaten Geoff. I got out just in time to see you lunge for him. You were so drunk though, he just stepped to one side and you slammed straight into the wall. Then you threw up all over him and started to ask Michelle why she didn't love you. With all the vomit trickling out of your mouth it wasn't hard to see why. Geoff was about to beat you up when Jimmy arrived and calmed things down. Becky was with him as well. She was really nice. Michelle said something to her and at one point they both nearly had a fight but Jimmy convinced Geoff to take Michelle inside and then carried you back here. A few of the kids were filming it on their phones. It'll be on Facebook by now I'd imagine. And YouTube. And whatever else the kids put clips on. Anyway, once Jimmy and Becky helped you upstairs, you refused to lie down in the bed and then just started to vomit again, only now it was just some kind of black stuff. I think it melted the carpet. I don't know why you drink so much. I could never embarrass myself like that. I just couldn't. Lord only knows how you're going to face the neighbours."

Oh god.

I spent a few hours staring into space, trying and failing to feel better. My mum left me alone and the dog still wouldn't come near me. At half six, Jimmy phoned up and asked me how I was. I told him and he proceeded to tell me everything my mum had already told me. Twice. He seemed to be gloating.

Sometimes, your friends can be very, very cruel.

Another hour passed as I tried to remember the previous night's events. My memory stopped around the time I met Charlie with the stolen games console. I tried not to think about that on the grounds it made me feel scared. Paranoid, I phoned John up at the Hope and asked him if he'd seen Charlie. He hadn't. I had a vague memory of hearing police sirens and getting chased by an Alsatian.

Was I a wanted man?

As for the other stuff, I just couldn't believe any of it. Mixing so much whisky with the dope had done it. It always fucked me up. I thought I'd learned. But then again, I had been under a lot of pressure.

I decided to never leave the house again.

It would be safer that way.

Half an hour later I was risking the outside world. My mum had gone to see a friend and there was no Coke or Pepsi in the house. I needed some Coke to settle my stomach and it was only a quick walk to the nearest shop. I took very small, careful steps and cut down an alley hoping to avoid anyone and everyone.

Footsteps behind me. Two people. I turned. Something hard

hit my head. I fell down. I looked up to see two figures. They could've have had others with them. I couldn't tell. Blood was starting to fill my eyes. My vision already shot.

"Take that, you pathetic fuck!" a familiar voice yelled.

I tried to trip one of them up but missed. One of the kicks hit my face. Blood started to run down my forehead…

… and then there was nothing.

It was all kind of hazy. A nurse melted out of darkness and asked me a few questions. She pulled out a pencil and drew a little picture of my face on some notes and pointed out where the bruises were. My whole body felt like shit. Every breath hurt. A doctor explained that the pain would come later, so that was something to look forward to. No one knew what happened, but it looked like I'd been mugged. I could remember leaving the house and turning into an alley, but nothing else. There was a boot coming towards my face, but that was all. I hated the fact that I couldn't tell the police anything. I'd never really thought about the police one way or the other but suddenly decided they were excellent and would be my very own avenging angels. Jimmy and Gabriel visited – together! Gabriel seemed to know one of the officers very well and this seemed to annoy Jimmy, but I couldn't be sure as I dozed off just after they arrived. I wasn't much help to them anyway.

No one could work out exactly how long I'd been in the alley unconscious. The first anyone knew of the mugging was when I'd staggered into the kitchen and proudly announced that I had one hell of a hangover before collapsing onto the table. My mum

had screamed and dropped the shopping she'd just bought –
which included a bottle of Coke. An ambulance was called and
I woke in hospital, unable to remember anything. I was told
to stay in overnight in case I had concussion. When I thanked
both the doctors and remarked on the twin nurses, they decided
I should stay for two nights.

The next day, I looked in a mirror and I realised just how
fucked I was. My face was one big bruise with two nasty cuts
near the right eye. They'd had to give me stitches on my forehead,
where something had cut me open. The doctor said that the scar
wouldn't be that bad. Maybe it was time to grow a fringe again.
My smile wasn't much better than the rest of my face – like some
rabid hillbilly's. The nurse said I'd been lucky. No broken bones,
just a few bruised ribs and a sprained ankle. There was a bandage
over the back of my head as well. One of the policemen said it
looked like someone had hit me from behind. A cute nurse told
me I was tougher than I looked. Nice to know someone had
finally noticed. The second day was better. There was more pain
but at least I could think straight. I just wanted to get out of the
hospital.

Too many memories and none of them good.

Visitors, loads of them. Mum and Dad – together. Jimmy,
Gabriel and Becky, John and few guys from the Hope. Jimmy
kept stressing that they were just friends, but every time he said
that, Gabriel looked a little hurt. Becky seemed really concerned
about me as well. Didn't know I had so many friends. And all of
them refused to stop talking. Which was a fucking pain 'cause

all I really wanted to do was sleep. John promised that if he heard who did me they'd be sorted. He was cool and even gave my mum a lift home. Jimmy was actually nice to me – not one sarcastic comment – well, maybe one, but it just slipped out. He was really trying to be nice, bless him.

And Becky…

Apparently she'd spent a few weeks in here with her kid when he'd first been born. Must have been a bad time for her.

The next day, my dad gave me a lift home – with my mum in the front. It was just like old times. Well, almost. The distance was still there – and an empty seat by my side.

We didn't talk much.

I spent most of the time sleeping. The doctor told me to take it easy for a couple of days. As soon as we got home, Happy ran up to me and started licking my hand. As I was going to sleep, I noticed he'd decided to stand guard at the foot of my bed.

The idea of sleeping for a very long time and waking up when I was feeling better was very appealing.

I slept for a few days, almost constantly, and was only vaguely aware of people coming to visit. I took a lot of very serious painkillers as, after a couple of days, my body started to realise it had been mugged and became one big sack of pain. On day three my phone buzzed. A Facebook update told me the happy news – Michelle and Geoff were engaged. Bollocks.

Eight

Stags, Love and a Kiss

"Here, this'll cheer you up," John said, handing me a free whisky.

I was in the Hope. After two weeks of lounging around the house, watching Marx Brothers films and Aussie soaps, I'd decided enough was enough and I had to rejoin the human race. I also figured getting out would be a good way to stop me thinking about the mugging. For the most part, I'd dealt with it pretty well. There were moments when I'd just freeze and feel terrified for no real reason at all, but those moments were getting fewer and fewer. The worst had been a few days after it had happened. I'd found myself almost possessed, pacing quickly around the back garden, convinced someone was after me. I got angry with myself and the world. Jimmy said it sounded like a panic attack. He used to get them a lot when he was a teenager and trying to work a few things out.

Talking to Jimmy helped a lot. He'd been beaten up three

times over the years – mainly by locals who weren't happy about his sexuality – so I guess he knew what he was talking about. It was Jimmy who'd urged me to get out in to the real world – or at least to the Hope.

"I'll tell you what's happened to Charlie. Even by his standards this is weird…"

"When you say weird, how weird? I mean I'm still recovering from the time he told me about the two Doberman dogs trying to lick his balls while he was having his way with that woman he met in job club."

"We all are," John said. "No, this isn't quite that gross, but still. Well, you know Charlie likes the odd dirty movie?"

"I've heard he considers himself a connoisseur. Always going on about them."

"Quite. Well, the other night his Lil was out babysitting – I know, I wouldn't let her within a country mile of any kid of mine, but each to their own – and Charlie had the flat to himself. So he got some blow – powerful stuff by all accounts – and one of his special DVDs and started to watch it. *Chateau du Passion,* apparently. Anyway, for once he's watched more than three minutes of it when he gets a text from Lil saying she's coming back with the kid and he should stick the kettle on. Worried about the kid seeing his drugs and porn, he quickly stuck them in a carrier bag and went to put them on a shelf – standing on one of his kitchen chairs to do so – when the chair collapsed and he found himself lying on the floor unconscious with a bag of drugs and porn on his chest. At which point the kid came in and woke him up while trying to look at one of the DVDs."

"Nasty," I smiled, accepting another Jack and Coke from John.

"That wasn't the end of it, though. He took his bag into the bedroom and popped down here for a quick one. Lil was in the kitchen making friends with her secret bottle of gin and had stuck the kid in front of the TV to watch *Shane the Chef* or something. It was hot, too, and they had all the windows open. Anyway, the kid pressed play and, instead of *Shane the Chef* appearing on the screen, something else did… Charlie had left the fucking DVD in the player. It came on at full blast too. Lil came rushing in here – dragging the poor kid behind her – and gave Charlie a real belt and made him get rid of all his porn. He'd been collecting it for years, too."

"Please don't tell me you took it off his hands?"

"Well, you know me, always willing to help a friend."

"Are you sure you want to touch something that Charlie's had his hands on after, how shall I say this, he's pleasured himself?" I asked.

John turned slightly pale and looked a little upset.

"Oh bloody hell. You've ruined it for me now."

"Alright, Billy?" Chrissie smiled, walking towards John. "What are you guys talking about?"

"Just lads' stuff." John said, turning a little red.

"If it's to do with that bag of porn you came back from Charlie's with, you should probably hide it before your mum gets back from the bingo."

"Good point," John said.

"You going to Lee's stag do later?" Chrissie asked me.

"Wouldn't miss it," I replied, secretly wishing I could just stay at home in bed.

"Do me a favour and make sure John and the gang don't damage my Lee. I'm marrying him on Saturday and I'd like him in one piece."

"I keep telling you, Chrissie, it's just a celebration of Lee's last night of freedom," John grinned, ducking a playful slap from Chrissie.

"I'm not sure Ste Norton's wife would think the same about his stag night."

"That was just a one-off, and anyway he was out of hospital in time for the wedding."

"Maybe, but just be careful, that's all I'm asking."

"You the boss?" a delivery driver asked.

John nodded.

"Good, I got a truckload of sand outside. Where do you want it dumping?"

"In here," John answered.

"Listen Billy, I hate doin' this to you but d'you mind buggerin' off for a while? I got a little surprise I want to prepare for tonight and I don't want anyone to know about it till it's the right time."

"Sure," I answered, as the driver and another guy started to carry bags of sand into the bar. "See you later."

I decided to stop off at Jimmy's on the way home. I was oblivious to everything and replaying a little scene in my head. It was a good scene where I sorted out the muggers and rewrote history. This time, when they jumped me, I was sober and holding a brick. I turned quickly and smashed the brick into the side of a face before kicking the second in the balls. When they were both on their knees, begging for forgiveness, I moved forward and used the brick to beat the living shit out of them. It felt good. It felt better than good. It felt great.

"You okay?"

"Huh?"

"You've got a weird smile on your face that, frankly, is quite disconcerting," Jimmy said.

"Sorry," I answered, following him into his house. "I was just daydreaming about smashing a brick into the cunts who mugged me."

"Fair enough," Jimmy answered. "Tea?"

I nodded and glanced around his living room.

"Place is clean…" I said.

Jimmy's place was never clean. He used to call it Bohemian Chic when he was drunk or stoned but really he just couldn't be arsed tidying up. But now…

"You've dusted," I said.

"I can dust," he replied, a little defensively. "Anyway, any joy remembering who jumped you?"

"No," I answered. "And stop changing the subject. The place is clean. Really clean. That can only mean one thing. Who's the lucky fella?"

"Remind me, why are we friends?" Jimmy asked, handing me a mug of tea.

"Because we've known each other for too long not to be," I answered. "I should really make an effort to find another friend, but to be honest it's just too much like hard work."

"That is true," Jimmy smiled. "Lord knows I've tried."

I raised an eyebrow.

"Okay," he said. "Gabriel's coming over and I might be a little nervous, okay? It's been ages since I had a drink with someone I actually liked."

"I have been meaning to have a word with you about your terrible dating choices…"

"Says the man who vomited over the last girl he fancied…"

"Nearly vomited…" I corrected. "There's a big difference between vomiting over someone and nearly vomiting over someone."

"I'm not sure Michelle would agree," Jimmy smiled. "Though considering who she's engaged to…"

"I know, can you believe it?" I answered. "And with me still single…"

"Did you know little Johnny has uploaded his footage of the night in question to YouTube? It's had a thousand hits."

"Good job I've decided to give up dating for a while…" I said, looking at my cup. "Got anything stronger?"

"Wine in the fridge," he answered. "Help yourself."

I came back with the bottle and a couple of glasses.

"You know, I quite envy you," I said, handing Jimmy a large glass of wine.

Jimmy gave me one of his looks. "Should I tell Gabriel?"

"I'm trying to be nice," I said. "Gabriel seems like a nice guy and you're one of the best people I know. You need to cut yourself some slack. It's about time you met someone good."

"I'm sorry, what have you done with my friend?" Jimmy smiled, uneasy with the compliment.

"I'm being serious," I said.

"I know," Jimmy smiled again.

"You deserve someone good."

Jimmy paused.

"Are we having a moment?" he grinned.

"You're such a wanker," I laughed.

"I'm sorry," Jimmy said. "Just nervous about tonight. And you're right. I do deserve someone good. We both do."

We clinked glasses.

"So," I said after a few moments' friendly silence. "Becky seems very cool."

"She *is* very cool," Jimmy said. "And a really nice person with a heart of gold. So totally not your type."

I pretended to be shocked.

"Anyway, it doesn't matter. Like I said, I've given up all that love stuff for a while."

"I'm getting a strange sense of déjà vu about this conversation," Jimmy grinned.

"I know, me too. And that's the problem. Anyway, looking like this I'm guessing it'll be a while before I get the chance…"

"Oh I don't know. It gives you a sort of rugged charm."

"Maybe," I said, suddenly feeling the darkness creeping back.

There was an awkward pause in the conversation as I contemplated the ultimate emptiness of existence and how everything any of us do was always going to end up in abject failure, misery or death. And possibly not in that order…

Jimmy let out a sigh and filled our glasses.

"Okay, if I tell you this, you cannot tell her, okay?" Jimmy said.

A little confused, I nodded.

"Becky was asking after you. I've tried to warn her, but who listens to me?"

"Sorry, did you say something?" I joked, secretly thrilled that "Becky had been asking after me. What was I – a six-year-old? "Maybe we should both have a go at dating people we actually like. Just for a change."

"I'll drink to that," Jimmy said.

By eight o'clock I was already drunk and at Lee's stag night. By nine I was very drunk and by ten I was exceptionally happy – albeit in a slightly wobbly kind of way. All the sand I'd seen delivered that morning had been for the party. John had decided to have a theme for the night. Some might've said he'd gone a little overboard, as the whole place had been turned into an exotic beach scene. Well, as exotic as pubs like the Hope could get with the addition of sand, fake palm trees and some blue paper as a pretend ocean. I don't think there was one sober person in the whole pub – although obviously my sober-finding powers were not at their peak. The world was starting to blur as time zoomed in and out of focus. I'm fairly sure I enjoyed myself and definitely talked a great deal of total bullshit. A policewoman walked in at one point and scared the life out of Charlie, who'd decided to come out of hiding for the stag do. She looked quite sternly at him, before turning her attention to Lee. He laughed, guessing what she was straight away. An instant later, she started peeling her clothes off. Strippers always make me feel embarrassed. The crowd went wild, though. I found it more fun watching them. A sixteen-year-old kid was getting extremely overexcited at the front and was on the verge of having his first sexual experience. Lots of blokes had formed a semicircle around her to admire the routine. Behind them, an old man was standing on a stool to get a better view. A few of his teeth were missing and his eyes had a weird and rather scary hunger to them. As the stripper removed her knickers, it all proved too much for him and he fell off the stool, smashing his face into the nearby bar. Within seconds he was back standing on his barstool, holding a tissue under his smashed nose and drinking his beer – which he hadn't spilt a drop of. As the stripper removed one of her high heels for her party piece, the testosterone level shot through the roof. The teenager was almost bent double as she finished her first act. With a final, dramatic pelvic movement, she threw the shoe to one side and approached a leering and swaying Lee. Some bloke with muscles who was clearly there as protection handed her a blindfold, which she placed on Lee before making him lick whipped cream off her slightly saggy but exceptionally large breasts. There was a lot of laughter at this and Lee seemed to overcome his normal dislike of dairy products. I guess I was getting rat-arsed again because the next thing I knew another hour had gone and I was slumped at a table talking to him. Lee was even drunker than me and still had traces of whipped cream on his face.

"You know something?" he slurred.

"What?" I replied. Not altogether certain the word had actually left my mouth.

"I really love Chrissie. I wouldn't tell the others 'cause they'd take the piss but you, you're a bit more…" He paused for a moment before continuing. "You're a bit more in touch with your effeminate side. I mean you've got A-levels and your best mate's an arse-bandit. No offence. But the others, they just don't understand what it's like to love."

"Hey, Lee!" John yelled from behind the bar. "Can I have you over here for a moment? It's time for the toast."

Lee staggered towards his older brother and started to grin as the whole pub cheered.

"Can I have some order?" one of the temporary bar staff shouted, to no avail.

"Shut up!" John yelled.

Everyone in the pub did just that.

"Now Lee's gettin' hitched in a few days to Chrissie – a lovely girl. And I think we all want to wish them the very best."

We all shouted in drunken agreement, some banging on the tables.

"Now, as you know, we have a little tradition in this pub," John continued.

Lee went a little pale.

"Whenever someone has a stag night, we do something special for them. For several years, we stripped the guest of honour naked, covered them in baby lotion and tied them to a lamp post. Unfortunately, after what happened to Graham, God rest his soul, we had to stop that. For a while we just got them drunk and stuck 'em in a hotel room with a sheep in garters. The RSPCA put a stop to that one."

"Bastards!" a thin guy called Phil heckled.

Lee knew what coming and smiled. He thought he was safe.

"So, for the last eighteen months we've celebrated stag nights with the ritual shaving of the groom's head. Of course, all the previous grooms have been kind enough to have hair. As a few of you may have noticed, my kid brother doesn't have any."

Lee was grinning, convinced he'd gotten away with it. I should have told him about Life and the baseball bat.

"In fact, I have it on very good authority my brother doesn't have a single hair anywhere on his body," John said, as a couple of big fuckers moved forward and stood either side of Lee. "That presented us with a bit of a problem."

My heart went out to Lee and I made a mental note never to get married.

"Now, we considered a few things. Pete thought we should club Lee unconscious and leave him tied naked to a tree in Aberystwyth. As he's always been jealous of Lee and Chrissie, and this plan would possibly result in Lee's death, we decided against it. Especially when we realised we'd all be too pissed to drive to Aberystwyth. We then considered the possibility of dressing him up as a baby and leaving him outside his mother-in-law's. Again, we decided against this as his mother-in-law is quite scary. Indeed, at one point it seemed we had reached an impasse."

John paused for dramatic effect.

"But then, watching an old episode of *Top of the Pops*, the answer came to me like an answer to my own personal S.O.S."

On cue, Abba's *S.O.S.* started playing loudly on the jukebox. The blokes grabbed Lee's arms. He struggled, but they were too big – even for Lee.

"It is time to give Lee a makeover – nineteen seventies' style." John produced a woman's ginger wig from the mid seventies and a tube of superglue. Within seconds, the wig was firmly stuck to Lee's head and one of the other drunks was adding a bit of lipstick to his face. A few minutes later, Lee looked like a cross between the Joker and a reject from *The Rocky Horror Picture Show.*

Everyone cheered. Lee looked straight at me, an expression of desperation etched on his face. I smiled weakly, and then Lee was handed a massive bucket of ale to down in one. I looked across the pub and saw my film-making mate Barry sitting alone at a table, a glass of orange juice in front of him. I raised my glass and for a moment he almost smiled. An instant later, Lee sort of melted into the seat next to me, the wig still firmly glued to his head, some cream still around his mouth. Both eyes seemed to be spinning out of control.

"You gotta laugh," he said, before promptly passing out.

One of his mates from the local rugby team suddenly produced some baby clothes and other members of the team decided that it might be fun to leave him outside his mother-in-law's after all.

I decided enough was enough. If I was going to make it home in one piece, it was time to leave.

And besides, I really needed a kebab.

I was eating a House Special and singing an old song of Jimmy's to myself as I turned the corner into my road.

"Can I have some?" a voice asked from behind me.

I nearly jumped out of my skin before recognising the voice as Becky's.

"I've just been to Chrissie's hen party," she stated, taking some kebab meat. "Don't tell anyone, but I'm a little pissed."

She seemed to be irritated at having told me this and looked away for a few moments.

"Know the feelin'," I nodded, wobbling about a bit.

"How… how are you?" she asked.

"Fine," I replied, slowly rocking back and forth. "How's…?"

I couldn't remember her kid's name. Oh god, what a scumbag. Here I was talking to a neighbour, what's more, someone I was really starting to like – with really nice eyes – and I couldn't remember the name of her kid. What sort of shallow bastard was I!?

"…the kid?" I finished, hoping she wouldn't ask me his name.

"He's fine. Thinks he's Spider-Man at the moment."

We fell silent for a while and started to look at everything but each other.

A billion stars were shining down on us.

"It's a beautiful night," she mumbled, more to herself than me.

"Yeah," I said, staring at the side of her face.

I looked away as she turned to face me.

"Billy…?" she almost whispered nervously. "Have you ever… I mean do you ever want… what I'm trying to say is that, well if…"

She trailed off and seemed a little embarrassed. We caught each other's eyes and smiled and then looked away quickly.

A thought was hiding at the back of my heart but I couldn't quite place it.

"Oh sod it," she said, and kissed me.

It was a good kiss. It was so good I dropped the kebab. It lasted for quite some time. The world started to spin and fireworks appeared in the night sky. We never stopped kissing, and then she broke away and was almost in tears.

"I'm sorry. I didn't… I mean, I know how you feel about Michelle and everything. Oh bloody hell!"

With that, she faded quickly into the night. Not allowing me the time to say anything.

Not allowing me the time to say how much I enjoyed the kiss.

I remained in the street for a while, trying to work things out. I didn't seem to be drunk anymore. That struck me as odd. I did feel weird though. My fingers touched my lips. The taste of her was still with me. Too many thoughts were filling my head.

Becky had kissed me. It was a good kiss. It was a wonderful kiss. Did this mean she liked me? How did I feel? Would Liverpool ever win the league again? She was great. I hardly knew her. Why did I feel so light-headed?

For a few insane moments I thought about knocking on her door and trying to talk to her. I thought of taking her in my arms and kissing her again…

But then the alcohol came back and I remembered that I was drunk and it was still only a month or so since I'd made a total prick out of myself with Michelle. I was probably getting my signals crossed. Becky was probably just drunk. Or it was some kind of joke.

Totally fucking confused, I went home and headed straight for bed. I drifted off to sleep with Becky dancing through my thoughts.

Nine

Graves, Rain and Chances

The sun was shining through my window. I didn't bother trying to get back to sleep even though it was early. I just stayed in bed staring out at the bright blue sky, thinking about the world and my life and Becky.

Becky.

I smiled every time I thought of her. Michelle was a name from my past.

The kiss.

The kiss had been good. I thought about it and smiled some more.

Becky.

Later, I went to visit Jenny. I took her some flowers and cleared some of the weeds from her grave. The date on the headstone didn't seem to be real.

Five years had passed since she died.

It felt like nothing had changed.

It felt like everything had changed.

Sometimes I'd chat to her. Not out loud or anything mad like that, but in my mind. Somehow that seemed okay. Like she could hear me. I knew she was dead but...

I missed her so much.

She'd been a rainbow. A living, breathing rainbow. Too young for life to beat and make cynical. Too young to know anything other than the simple joy of being alive. My thoughts were becoming grim. They always did standing by her grave. Time slipped back to when she was alive, when Mum and Dad were together and I had a job at a record shop in town. Jenny used to run out to meet me when I came home. She'd tell me just about everything that had happened to her since breakfast and a whole lot more. I'd like to say I listened to every precious word, but I didn't. Sometimes... sometimes I was even bored and wished she'd just leave me alone. Standing by her grave, I'd have given anything just to see her face, hear her voice just one more time.

It's been a weird few weeks, I told her. I've been mugged, drunk and now... now I'm thinking about Becky a lot. You never met her, but I think you'd like her. She's cool. She's strong as well. Independent. I like that. It makes a change after some of the women I've known. Mum's fine. So's Dad. He's having a baby.

I know.

You do? Yeah, I guess you would do. Hope you're okay.

I'm fine. Don't worry.

What's it like where you are?

Lovely. You remember that book you bought me, the one set in the seaside one summer? It's like that but with more people and less crowds. Granddad's here and loads of other people. You'd love it.

That's good. I miss you.

I miss you too.

I closed my eyes and felt like the last person on Earth. All my friends had been taken from me and I missed them all. Nothing was good and everything was going to end in pain, suffering and misery.

Don't be stupid, her voice whispered.

Could someone be haunted by memories?

Jenny was lying on the couch. The old, golden couch my folks used to have in the living room. She was a few days old and my Mum had just brought her back from the hospital. She was this little innocent bundle of hope and love and possibilities. Her eyes were still closed and her hands so small it almost caused my heart to crack. She seemed to be pulling faces, as though she was trying to work out what was going on and where she was and what everything did.

And then, an instant later, she was learning to walk. Holding the walls and sofa and anything else she could find to help balance herself and follow me and Mum all the time. When we went in to the kitchen, the gap between the lounge and the kitchen became a chasm to her. She'd lean against the far wall for support, a single small arm stretching out across the gap to the kitchen doorway, as she made gurgling noises to me or Mum.

"Listen," she'd say. "I could walk. I could just let go of this wall and keep going across this gap. I really could. I'm just not gonna bother today. That's all. Okay?"

Of course, it came out as a series of weird baby noises, but we understood her perfectly. A lot of the time, the noises she made sounded strangely like "Billy".

Later, when she had just about got the hang of walking, she managed to climb the first step of the staircase. Usually there was a guard up, but that day someone had left it off. The struggle it must have taken to clamber up that step was immense and, as I rushed over to stop her climbing any further, she glanced back at me and smiled one of the ten greatest smiles of all time before deciding to have a sit-down, forgetting that there was nothing but air behind her. She fell off the stairs and froze on the floor, looking at me again as if to say "Fuck!", her lower lip quivering before she burst into tears.

And later and later still...

Too many memories.

Too much emotion.

It was one of the reasons I didn't visit the grave that often. It was just too painful. And I couldn't help thinking that somewhere along the way we all had to forget about the pain and the loss and try to carry on. I couldn't for the longest of times. Life was just black. With Jenny dead and the nature of her death… I had a lot of hate in me. Too much for my own good. I still did five years later but tried not to dwell on it. Preferring to think of positive things. Of the possibilities life could bring. It was what Jenny would've wanted. Somewhere Jenny watched and agreed. At least it felt like she did. I sank to my knees and traced her name with my fingers. A light rain started to drift down from the heavens. It didn't bother me. Somehow rain and graveyards went together.

I stayed there for a while, not really thinking about anything.

My eye was eventually drawn to an old oak tree behind her headstone. She'd always liked trees. When she was learning to talk, she used to walk around repeating that one word over and over again: "Tree, tree, tree," like some personal mantra.

"Tree," I whispered, rising to my feet. As I did, I was stunned to see Becky standing in front of a grave a short distance away. She placed some flowers on the cold, damp earth and started to walk slowly towards me, smiling weakly when she got closer.

Her eyes were puffed and bloodshot. She'd been crying. She looked like a ghost. A sad, beautiful ghost.

"I didn't expect to see you," I smiled. "Do you come here often?"

"Not as often as I should," she whispered.

Without saying anything else we started walking out of the graveyard. It was almost as though we didn't want to talk before we passed through the gate and left the dead and our thoughts behind. As we turned onto the road, the rain stopped.

"Are you okay?" I asked.

Usually uncomfortable with emotion, I was surprised at the sincerity behind my words. Something was happening and I was totally helpless before it.

"Yeah, I just… Jack's father, he… well, there was this car crash and…"

"Christ, I didn't know…"

"It was a few years ago. Just before Jack was born."

"Shit."

More silence. It didn't matter. I thought of her pregnant, her lover dying, the baby in hospital. I thought of all these things and more and my heart started to bleed for her.

"Jenny, my sister. She's buried there. Five years now but I still… sometimes I just feel…"

"I know. Me too."

We seemed content just to walk for a while. The sun was starting to push its way through the grey clouds as we turned into the park.

"I remember years ago walking through here with Jenny. She was about eight and mad about ducks. Every time we walked through the park we'd have to take any crumbs we could find to feed them. This one time she somehow smuggled a whole loaf out to give them. When my mum complained, Jenny just said that it didn't seem fair to make the ducks eat stale bread all the time. She said it with such an earnest face, we fell about laughing. Course, that just made Jenny sulk. She looked so cute when she sulked…"

"I wish I'd known her," Becky said, smiling faintly.

Somehow I knew she meant it and that they were not just empty words of kindness.

"She'd have liked you."

"When Jack's father died, I didn't know what to do. For a while things got pretty bad. I got pretty bad. You ever have times like that?" Becky turned to look at me and set off a firework display in my soul.

"Yeah…"

We paused by the lake. Both smiling as we saw a couple of ducks floating by.

"When Jenny died. A few months after… long after everyone had stopped asking me how I felt, I just… it was almost like life left me for a while and I was nothing. Not even a shell. Just some walking mess of flesh and blood. I just… there was nothing. I felt physically ill, I was convinced I had some disease, some cancer eating away at me. At my soul. Sometimes I even thought about killing myself. I know, now it doesn't make sense. Now I look around and think how could I even contemplate leaving this…" I motioned around the park with my arms and then, catching sight of the chimneys in the distance, added, "Well, maybe not this, but you know what I mean. Life in general. Back then though… back then there was nothing. I came here a few times and I was just empty. Emotionless. Anything good. Everything good – music, friends, nature, none of it touched me. My sister was dead. My parents were about to divorce and life was black. One weekend I was consumed with the concept of my own mortality. I didn't see a point in anything. Life was all about suffering. Things were bad and would only get worse, so why prolong the suffering? On the Sunday, around sunset, I was walking through the park on the way to a friend's house, listening to a few songs on my phone. One of them was by a group called The Church. A song called "Tear It All Away". Anyway, it was a cool evening and all of a sudden I was consumed with this great feeling of being alive. I mean, we all get these feelings but sometimes we lose track of them. I had. I stopped walking for a while, listened to this guitar solo in the song as the sun set over the factories. It was right here. Where I'd stood so many times with Jenny. Everything suddenly looked so beautiful, so alive. For no reason I could think of at the time, tears just started to stream down my face. I knew then that, no matter what happened, it was all worth while and that somewhere I was still talking to Jenny. I mean, time itself is a man-made concept. I came to this park with Jenny six years ago. Stood here with her in this very spot and somehow we're still here. We always *will* be here – in that moment. And others. She's still alive, somewhere in the past… and I'm rambling. Sorry."

"No, it's alright… I know what you mean."

I smiled and found myself staring at Becky and realised that I was smiling because I was looking at Becky and then I found myself picturing the two of us rolling around naked together and blushed and decided to look at the lake for a while.

"It's getting cold," she smiled.

I couldn't help feeling that she knew what I was thinking, and blushed again.

"I usually stop off for a drink on the way home," she explained. "Just to… well, just to get my head back together…"

"Mind if I join you?" I asked, trying to make it sound innocent and nothing like a date. After all, you couldn't ask people on a date shortly after leaving a graveyard. It just wasn't done.

"I was just about to ask…" she smiled.

It was one hell of smile.

The kind that crept right under your skin and straight into your bloodstream.

We didn't talk much on the way to the pub.

We didn't need to.

"So I'm trying to get the money together to start a stall. In that new market they've opened. I know it's filled with hippies, but they're not all that bad and it'd give me a chance to clear out some stuff."

"Like what?" I asked.

It was a few hours later and we'd been drinking and talking

ever since leaving the graveyard. It felt good. Neither of us mentioned the night before. We didn't need to. Somehow it had only served to make us close with what seemed like amazing speed. I was more than happy just listening to her talk, and desperately trying to remember every word.

"Clothes, records. Back in my younger days I was a bit of a Goth. Total black look, pierced nose, big, black boots and all the vinyl to match. Siouxsie and the Banshees, The Cure. I'm still a big Cure fan."

"They're a good band."

"Met Robert Smith once."

"No!"

"Yeah, we bluffed our way backstage and managed to hang out with them for a while. Worst thing was I really fancied him at the time. I mean, I was seventeen and I thought he was so cool. Even with all that hair."

"You didn't…"

"No, I didn't. But my best friend Tina did – with one of the guitarists. She was always doing that. Used to drive me nuts. Every time we went out, all the good-looking guys would flock to her and I'd be left with their dumb mates who were so shy they could hardly speak."

"What happened to her?"

"She has a lot of bad luck – especially with men. The last one she met was at a club in town. She took him home, had her wicked way with him, only to be told first thing in the morning that he had to be off 'cause he was getting married. He even invited her to the wedding. In fact, I think they even, well…"

I coughed up my drink.

"So she's a little loose?" I smiled.

"Just a little."

"Got her number?"

Becky kicked me under the table. It was a good kick. A playful kick. We fell silent for a while and concentrated on our drinks. A few thousand years were spent stealing glances at her.

"Something wrong, you seem to be miles away?" Becky asked, bringing me back to earth.

"I was just thinking… it's weird, you've lived in the same street for over a year but I don't really know you. I mean, I only ever saw you as Bullion's girlfriend."

"Please, don't mention him."

"Why?"

"It's a sore point. Listen, I'm not sure I should tell you this. I mean, I still don't really know you, but I feel like I do. If that makes sense? Anyway, Jeremy was the first, how can I put this?"

As she started to explain her relationship with Jez, and for the first time in my life, I envied him – and hated him all the more for that.

"Okay, when I was fourteen, I really liked him. We must have been together for about three years but then we drifted apart. He met Sarah and I ended up with Jack's father. Jeremy turned up just after… the car crash and for a while he was great. Took care of me when I needed it, but after Jack was born he changed. Don't know if he was jealous or what, but it just didn't work out. I still like the guy – it's all right, no need to look so worried, I know you two hate each other – but he does have a good side…"

I'd never considered the possibility that Jez had a good side. The thought of it was totally unsettling.

"You know what it's like. I met him when I was fourteen. It's an impressionable age. He was the first guy I got drunk with, smoked dope with and, well, you know. Everyone's got someone like that back then."

I smiled weakly. At fourteen I was locked in my room reading comics and listening to really loud and depressing music.

"Okay, I can understand most of that, but Bullion? I can't believe he has a good side."

"You can talk," Becky smiled. "Michelle?"

There was a mischievous light in her green eyes.

"I'm beginning to wonder what I saw in her. It's just…" I paused for a moment and finished my drink. "You know, it'd be great to meet someone with no complications, wouldn't it? Someone you could actually find attractive and get on with and not have any of the other hassles."

"Yeah, it would, wouldn't it?" Becky answered, glancing at her drink.

For a second I thought I caught her looking at me, but she was just staring quietly at her glass.

"I've just got to call my mum, see how Jack is," she said, pulling a mobile phone from her handbag. "I said I'd be back by now."

As she talked on the phone, I seized the chance to get a good bit of staring in. She really was beautiful. She'd dyed the ends of her black hair a purple colour today. Her face was both delicate and strong, radiating energy and hope. She had only the faintest traces of make-up on and for some reason her skin reminded me of spring. Her lips were the most kissable I'd ever… I stopped the chain of thought. I'd been there before and it wasn't good.

Last time I'd been there, I'd ended up vomiting over some girl's boyfriend at two in the morning.

We were just friends.

Just friends.

Her breasts were moving softly under her jumper as she breathed.

"Is something wrong?" she asked, putting the phone back in her handbag.

"What?" I mumbled, shaking my head a little and trying not to look at her jumper.

"You look a little… flushed. Everything okay?"

She was concerned.

Excellent!

"Yeah, sorry. I was just thinking about… things."

She smiled and I again got the feeling she knew something I didn't.

"Anyway, I've got to get back. I don't like leaving Jack with Mum for too long. He's been a bit of a handful lately."

"I'll walk back with you, I said I'd nip in to have a chat with Jimmy anyway."

We talked all the way home and covered everything from favourite films to football teams. She was even a Liverpool fan.

As we neared the street, Becky stopped and faced me. I noticed that it was the same spot we'd met the night before.

Less than twenty hours before.

"Well, this is our street," I said, staring at the pavement.

A leaf drifted down past my gaze. The breeze stopped. Clocks ticked at half speed as time itself slowed down to allow us a moment. I looked up and Becky was smiling nervously.

"Listen, about last night. I just wanted to let you know…"

I kissed her. It seemed to say more than any words I could come up with.

She kissed me back.

We remained kissing for a very long time and then Jez appeared.

The weird thing was, and it really was weird, he didn't say a thing. He just stared at me. It wasn't a good stare and I couldn't help feeling that he was starting to find a whole new level of hatred for me.

So I returned his hate with a smile.

He mumbled something under his breath and walked away towards the bus stop.

"That probably wasn't good, was it?" I suggested, secretly overjoyed.

"Don't laugh," Becky warned, half pushing me away. "I should say something to him. Explain things."

Before she could reach him, he'd jumped on a bus and was gone.

"I've got to go," Becky said, walking down the road towards her house.

I ran after her and surprised myself with honesty that just came out of nowhere.

"Listen, I don't know what's going on, but something is. Can I see you sometime, maybe tonight?"

"I don't know. I…" she paused for a moment, "I can't tonight or tomorrow. I've got to take Jack to see his grandparents."

"No problem. How about when you get back?" I asked, trying to ignore the sense of urgency edging into my voice.

"Maybe," she half smiled, biting her lip and looking back towards the bus stop. "Call about eight and we'll do something… Oh. Hold on, it's Chrissie's wedding."

"Of course," I said, amazed that I'd forgotten all about it. "You are going, aren't you?"

She nodded.

"Alone?" I asked, hoping she'd nod again.

"Probably," she smiled.

"Probably?"

"Well, I'm hoping some guy I've met will ask me."

"Anyone I know?" I smiled. A little bit of me was worried I might not be the guy in question.

"Listen, if you don't ask me right now, I'll phone Tommy up and go with him."

"You know Mad Tommy?"

"I know more than you think I know. And you shouldn't call him mad, he's just a little touched."

"So do you want to go with me then?"

"Where to?" She smiled.

"The wedding."

"Okay. Call for me about one. Oh, actually it'd be better if I could meet you there, I want to drop Jack off with a mate for the afternoon."

"Look forward to it," I smiled.

And with that she was gone. I watched her walk up the path to her front door, trying to freeze-frame every sweet step she took and praying that once she reached the front door, she'd turn and wave. She did, and everything was good with the world. I closed my eyes and tried to capture everything.

It was a good moment.
One of the best.

Ten

Wigs, Weddings and Pizza

The wedding day started with me trying to coax Lee out of the toilet. It was nine thirty in the morning. A call from Annie Wayne had woken me up before first light, telling me I was needed and she'd explain everything when I arrived at the pub.

"What's happened?" I asked when I got there.

"Well…" John started to say, only to be interrupted by a slap on the head from his mum.

Annie Wayne might have been the wrong side of sixty but she was still terrifying when in a bad mood. About half the size of her two sons, I'd only seen her this angry on a couple of occasions before – when one of her clan had done something so stupid it was beyond belief.

"Ask smartarse here!" she snapped, scowling at John, who blushed furiously and decided to stare at his feet for a century or two. "It's all his fault."

"It was only a joke," John mumbled, only to receive another

clout from Mrs Wayne.

"A joke? A bloody joke!? Our Lee's locked himself in the bathroom because he's got an orange wig stuck on his head and you think it's funny!?"

"Well, it is in a way," John whispered.

His mum gave him a look that shrivelled him.

"I'll go and see if there's anything in the kitchen that might help," he said, quickly vanishing down the stairs.

"Make your friend a cup of tea while you're down there. It's the least you can do!" she yelled, leaving a ringing in my ears.

I smiled a little nervously, not sure what to say to the living hurricane standing next to me.

"Sorry about all this," she said, in her poshest voice. "But our John didn't know what to do and Lee said you were the only one who'd understand."

"No problem," I answered, wondering just what the hell I *could* do.

"So he's still got the wig on?" I asked.

"At first we all thought it was funny," Mrs Wayne answered. "But when it was still on yesterday, well... poor Lee's always been the sensitive one."

"I'm not coming out!" Lee's voice sulked from the other side of the door. "You'll have to tell Chrissie the wedding's off."

"Lee, it's Billy. Come out of there and we'll see what we can do. I'm sure there's some way of getting it off."

"There's not," Mrs Wayne said, rather unhelpfully. "We've tried everything. Warm soapy water, razor blades, grease. I even trimmed it to see if I could at least make it look half decent, but it didn't really work."

The bathroom door opened and it took all my self-control to stop myself from laughing.

Lee was dressed in his tux, but the shirt was hanging loose and his hair, or rather the wig, which had looked bad enough when it had originally been put on his head, now looked even worse. Most of the fake hair had been cut short, giving him a really naff ginger look – only bits had been pulled free of the cloth, revealing patches of the fabric beneath.

Lee's face was the most tragic I had ever seen.

"I hate to say this, Mrs Wayne, but I'd have to agree with your son on this one – there's no way he can get married looking like that."

"See. I knew Billy'd understand. He knows what I'm going through. He's in touch with his effeminate side, he is."

"However, I think I know someone who can help him. Do you mind if I call some friends?"

"If it gets him to the church on time, you can skin the cat and belt our John over the head with it."

Jimmy and Gabriel arrived ten minutes later. I'd put them up to speed with events and Gabriel turned up armed to the gills with chemicals, scrapers and scalpels.

"Now that is a mess," he said, enjoying the discomfort he seemed to be causing the Wayne brothers. Jimmy seemed more uncomfortable. He'd only met Lee and John a couple of times and never really got on with them due to their occasional bouts of rabid homophobia. I'd tried to explain that they weren't really bigoted, just class A piss-takers, but he hadn't agreed. Still, their mum was almost falling over herself to make them both feel at home.

"Don't worry," Gabriel said. "I'm sure I can fix it. Let's go into the bathroom and sort it out."

Lee looked horror-stricken at the prospect of this.

"Don't worry, dear. I don't bite," Gabriel said, putting on a ridiculously camp voice to wind Lee up. "At least not on first dates."

Everyone apart from Lee laughed, but he still followed Gabriel into the bathroom.

"This shouldn't take long," Gabriel said in his usual voice, accepting the tea Lee's mum had made.

The four of us remained outside the bathroom, glancing at each other sheepishly. Strange sounds came from behind the door. Scraping, sawing, whispering…

"Don't be such a big baby," Gabriel snapped at one point.

"He'll be fine," I said to John and his mum, who were starting to look more than a little worried.

"I'm sure Gabriel's done this sort of thing a thousand times before," Jimmy added.

"So," John said, trying his best to appear natural. "Have you two been, well, have you two known…"

"Just a month or so," Jimmy interrupted, saving John's blushes. "But I've known him for years. He helped Billy out a while back when he was having a bad hair day."

"It's a nice cut," John said.

"Thanks," I answered.

"More tea?" Mrs Wayne asked, even though we hadn't finished the first mugs.

The bathroom door opened slightly and Gabriel's head popped out.

"Could someone call an ambulance, please?" he asked.

Mrs Wayne went pale.

"Just kidding," Gabriel laughed, opening the door with a flourish and gesturing Lee out into the real world.

The wig was gone and Lee's head, while a little raw, no longer looked stupid.

"Now, if I was the groom," Gabriel said. "I'd let that dry for a little while and then add some make-up to cover the blotches. I'm afraid there's nothing I could do about that. Glue and skin should never mix."

"I'm not wearing make-up," Lee almost choked. "Everyone'd think I'm a puff. No offence."

"Trust me, no one would ever consider you a puff," Gabriel smiled.

That seemed to cheer Lee up no end.

"Well, we'd best be off then," Gabriel said, moving towards the stairs.

"Lee…" Mrs Wayne urged.

"You don't have to go," Lee said. "In fact, after all you've done I thought you might, y'know, want to come the wedding or something."

"Yeah," John added, less convincingly.

"Love to," Gabriel answered, before Jimmy could think of an excuse.

"Thanks again," Lee said, seeing us to the door.

Gabriel and Jimmy were already down the drive when Lee started to shake my hand.

"Thanks," he said. "I owe you for that."

"It was more Gabriel than me," I replied.

"Yeah, he's not bad for an arse bandit, is he?" Lee smiled.

I flinched a little, but at least it was a start.

They were just about to leave when Jimmy beckoned me over.

"I need a quick word about something."

"Sure, what's wrong?"

"Nothing. It's just that, well, I know you kissed Becky the other night and I know what you're like. You're my best friend, but Becky's become a good friend as well and she's had a lot to put up with and…"

"And you don't want me making things any worse for her?" I finished.

"Yeah, something like that."

"Listen, I don't know what's happening," I told him. "I honestly don't. All I know is that I've started to think a lot of her. And not in the way you're thinking. I promise you that I'll never do anything to hurt her. Anything. Now does that make you feel better?"

"Not really," he replied with half a smile. "But I guess it'll have to do. Who knows, maybe the next wedding will be yours."

"I said I like Becky, I didn't say I wanted to marry her. Besides, I still think marriage is a punishment from God."

"You really need to get out more," Jimmy laughed. "I'll see you later."

"Sure," I said, as Jimmy climbed into Gabriel's car. It struck me again how at ease they seemed with each other. Would I be that happy with Becky? Would I get the chance to be?

I hoped so.

I felt I would be.

And I very nearly was.

The wedding itself went without a hitch. Lee must've taken Gabriel's advice about the make-up because as he stood at the front of the church, his head looked perfectly normal. In fact, it looked better than normal. Something a few people remarked on. John wasn't mad about his kid brother wearing make-up, but had to admit that it was probably for the best. I got there early, with Jimmy and Gabriel. Becky was coming from her friend's, who was looking after Jack for the day, and when she entered the church… well, when I die I'll have a few good memories and that will be one of them. She was beautiful. So beautiful my mind did a runner and she was the only thing left in my head. Jimmy later told me that my jaw dropped open and it well could have. He also nudged me into action and I stepped out to ask if she wanted to sit next to me. She did. Jimmy started smirking and there wasn't much I could do to stop him. A quick elbow from me just made him smirk even more. When Chrissie walked down the aisle I was in heaven. Not because I came over all soppy about the wedding but because it gave me a chance to stare at Becky while pretending to look at Chrissie. I think she noticed because when Chrissie reached the front, Becky turned to face me and seemed to be trying not to laugh.

"The wedding's that way," she whispered, her smile knowing way too much for its own good.

I blushed furiously.

"Go gently on him," Jimmy whispered to her across my body. "He's an idiot."

I was about to reply when some old dear behind me shushed Jimmy into silence. There's not much else to say about the wedding. I'm not religious but I had to admit that sitting there in the church started me thinking about things. Strange things like commitment and love and staying with someone for more than two months. It must be a good feeling, I thought, to know that you love someone so much you're willing to spend your whole life with them. Slowly removing the dress they're wearing for a wedding before… Wait, my own voice said, I cannot think about having sex with Becky while in a church. I might not have been religious but there had to be something wrong with that. I forced my mind to drift away from thoughts of Becky and onto other things. Thoughts about Life and the universe and pizzas. For some reason, I really felt like a pizza. Would I ever get married? I was nearly twenty-seven. How long could my life stay the same without getting really sad? One meaningless relationship after the other. Would I still be like that in my thirties or forties? Christ, I hoped not. I glanced around the church and tried not to think about God too much. Religion just depressed me. When I was a teenager, it used to make me angry. At one point there'd even been a rumour that the Catholic Brothers who ran the sixth form I'd attended wanted to burn me at the stake for heresy. I'm not sure if it was true but it might have been. I guess it had all started going wrong when I was ten and reading the stations of the cross in the local church. This was a traditional good old Catholic event where the kids from the local junior school used to stand up in front of a packed church and read. Back then, I had an excellent reading age and was never bothered about speaking in public so was always picked to go first. This one day, I was on the altar with eleven other kids from my class, waiting to do my piece. When the time came, I stepped up to the mike, showing no fear, to read the words

"The First Station of the Cross" off a little card in my hands. But instead of saying The First Station of the Cross, I said "The First Commandment". I knew I'd fucked up straight away but carried on reading regardless. No one seemed to notice and I thought I'd managed to get away with it. Until the next morning in assembly when I was sitting at the back of a packed school hall listening to the headmaster drone on.

"And congratulations to everyone who took part in last night's event. It all went very well – apart from William Cade's little mistake!"

The entire school – one hundred and thirty-three kids, six teachers and three dinner ladies – took that as the cue they needed to turn and laugh at me. I was ten and a half. All things considered, I handled it very well. I burst out crying and didn't stop for three hours. Maybe that was the start of my anti-religious sentiment. Or maybe it was just because I'd grown up.

The ceremony passed pretty quickly and whatever I was thinking about must've done the trick because, before I knew what was happening, Jimmy was nudging me again and everyone was leaving.

For a while, we just loitered outside while the photographer snapped away.

"It was a nice service," I said to Becky.

Jimmy giggled.

"James," Gabriel snapped.

"Sorry."

"What's so funny?" I asked.

"You are," Jimmy said.

"I don't know what you mean."

"Oh please."

"He's just being mean. Ignore him," Becky smiled. "Oh look, it's our turn."

And with that she slid her hand into mine. The suddenness of the movement took me by surprise and sent my heart cartwheeling around the other guests.

"Smile," the photographer said.

"No problem," I replied, looking straight at Becky.

We stayed holding hands for a long time.

It all really started at the reception. It was upstairs in the Hope and, needless to say, a lot of alcohol was consumed. At least that's what people told me. I spent the whole night with Becky. Talking and not talking. It was cool. Very cool. There were a few moments of weirdness. At one point some rugby player decided to pick a fight with a very drunk John. Obviously this was not a wise course of action, but before John could react to a rather badly swung punch, Gabriel had the guy in an armlock and kicked him out of the pub.

I only found this out later in the night when a drunk Jimmy staggered over to me.

"Look at that. Isn't it sweet?" he slurred.

He was carrying a pint of lager in his hand and downed the last of it before continuing. Well, he tried to down it. About half the pint missed his mouth and flowed down the side of his chin.

"When in Rome," he grinned, using all his skill to place the empty glass on the nearby table.

Becky smiled.

"I think Gabriel and John are bonding," Jimmy said, slumping down in the middle of us.

"Great," I answered with a forced smile. Until that moment, I'd been getting closer and closer to Becky. In my own head, I'd been about five seconds away from trying to kiss her. Jimmy had made that impossible.

"I'm not jealous or anything, though," Jimmy said, slumping back onto the bench. "'Cause if I was jealous that would be stupid because I don't want to get involved with anyone at the moment and it's not like he means anything to me or anything. Sorry, was I interrupting something?"

"No, course not," I said, sarcastically.

"Good," he replied, staring down at the table. "I feel pissed."

"You'd never guess," Becky smiled.

"You're lovely, you are," he slurred, using a hand to steady himself on our table. "So, has he made his move yet?"

"Not yet," Becky smiled. "We're just talking."

"He's a bit crap, isn't he?" Jimmy said, and then turning to me added, "She's crazy about you, you know. Has been for ages. And you like her, so why don't you do something about it?"

"Is he bothering you two?" Gabriel said, helping Jimmy to his feet. Jimmy draped an arm around Gabriel and pecked him on the cheek. Two old fogies nearby nearly fell off their stools at the sight.

"I think I should take him home," Gabriel said.

"Don't wanna go home," Jimmy sulked. "I wanna stay here and get pissed with the lads."

"You can't stand up, James," Gabriel pointed out.

"I can so," Jimmy answered, pushing his way free of Gabriel

and, after a quick wobble, managing to stand on his own.

"See!" he stated proudly, before collapsing on to the table in front of us. Beer splashed up all over Becky.

"Oops," Jimmy giggled, looking up from the floor.

"Come on," Gabriel laughed, pulling a rather rubbery Jimmy to his feet.

"Okay, officer."

"Sorry about Jimmy," Gabriel said to Becky, who was wiping beer off her dress.

"Don't worry," she smiled. "It's getting to be a habit. I was about to go anyway."

"You were?" I said.

"Yeah," she smiled. "If I can find someone to walk me."

"William, William…" Jimmy yelled, draping an arm over my shoulder and almost pulling me onto the floor.

"What?" I asked.

"This is your big chance. You can walk her home. I think she wants you to."

"Wow. Do you really think so?"

"You two take care," Gabriel smiled, leading Jimmy away.

"Give her one from me!" Jimmy yelled, forcing everyone to turn round and stare at the two of us.

"Listen, I really have to get home. I'm soaked," Becky said, rising to her feet.

"I should be going as well," I lied. "Mind if I walk you home?"

Her smile was the only answer I needed.

"Just one thing though," she said as we left. "Do you mind if we stop off for some food on the way back? I'm dying for a pizza."

It was a good pizza.

"Happy Christmas," she smiled after.

My heart was pounding and my soul was off doing the lambada. We were lying together in her bed, having made it there on the third attempt. Our first kiss had been in front of the TV. We'd been sitting on the floor, eating pizza and watching *Attack of the Fifty Foot Woman* while trying not to think about sex. I was still worried that she might not like me. The fact that she'd already kissed me and held my hand on the way home were pretty good arguments that she did but, at the same time, I couldn't shake the feeling that she secretly hated me and would soon turn and say, "Sorry, I thought you were someone else. Please go. You're the ugliest and most annoying person I've ever met."

Instead, she'd wiped some pizza from my mouth and kissed me again. The kiss had been followed by contact of a more intimate nature on the settee and carpet. After a bit more rolling around, she'd led me into bed. It was amazing. The sex I'd been having with other women suddenly didn't seem like real sex. And for once I didn't have the urge to run away.

"This is nice," I said, amazed at how beautiful she looked naked.

"I bet you say that to all the girls," Becky whispered, snuggling up closer to me.

He scent reminded me of everything that was good with the world. I breathed in and closed my eyes.

"Every one of them," I teased. "But this time I mean it. I…"

Becky kissed me again. I kissed her back.

For what seemed like ages, we didn't say anything. There was no need to.

The silence was amazing. At least to me. It felt like home. Like I'd spent all my life being this close to Becky.

The phone eventually broke the silence.

"I best get it," she said half apologetically to me. "It might be my mum."

"I'll keep the bed warm," I smiled, enjoying the sight of her bum as she walked into the living room.

"It's not a good time," I heard her say, her voice edged with a hint of anger.

"It's none of your business who's here and I don't care where you're going for Christmas."

Silence as the other person said something.

"Jeremy, I'm trying to be okay with this but you're not helping." Her voice was getting louder, she was almost shouting. "I told you the other week, I don't want to see you anymore. I'm sorry if that hurts you, but it's just the way it is."

The name took a few moments to hit home.

I rolled off the bed and poked my head around the corner. Becky was wiping a tear from her eye.

"Trouble?" I asked, probably a little too loudly.

Becky waved me away with a weak smile.

"Listen, Jeremy, I'm going to hang up. I'd like to stay friends, but if you can't deal with this like an adult, there's not much chance of that, is there? Yeah, well, same to you."

Becky slammed the receiver down.

"Sorry about that," she sniffed. "Probably not something you wanted to hear."

"You okay?" I asked, amazed to find out that I actually meant it. All thoughts of getting one over on Bullion gone at the sight of Becky upset.

"I'm fine," she sniffed. "It's just… Why are you men so stupid?"

"It's in the genes," I said, trying to make her feel better.

My mind was scrambling for ways of cheering her up. Making Becky happy seemed to be the only reason for my existence.

"I mean, Jeremy, it was over a long time ago but he just won't accept it and he was seeing other women. God, I hate him. We used to be friends as well. Phil was the same. He was fucking someone else. She even came to the funeral. That was the first I knew of it. Maybe it's me. Maybe I attract men who screw around."

"Hey, take it easy. I'm not like other men," I stepped closer and brushed a tear from her cheek. "And anyone who doesn't make you feel like the greatest person in the world is a total loser."

Becky sniffed a smile.

"Hell, I can't believe I'm here with you. I keep expecting God or someone to come down and tell me it was all a joke. Or maybe *Candid Camera* or something."

"They couldn't show it at peak time," she sniffed.

I pulled her close and for a while everything was good with the world.

Eleven

Love Scores a Hat-Trick

Some moments should last forever. A day in the park with Jenny, England beating Germany at football, lying in bed with Becky. For the next few days we were inseparable. I met her kid, Jack, and the two of us hit it off at once. He was a Liverpool fan and read the same comics I'd read as a kid. I gave him some of mine and bought him a big Scalextric set. Becky said I was spoiling him but didn't seem to mind that much. Jack even asked me to read him a bedtime story. My first attempt didn't go down too well. The whole idea of a bedtime story is to let kids drift off calmly into sleep, whereas mine had Jack running around his bedroom pretending to be a ghost. It soon became a regular thing – Jack to bed, nights with Becky. It all felt so natural. Then Christmas came. She was going away for a week to see Jack's grandparents and not coming back until New Year's Eve. A couple of days before Christmas we said our goodbyes and arranged to meet on New Year's Eve. I was missing her before she'd even left and saying goodbye broke my heart. The thought of being alone again terrified me – my new life with Becky was already so much better than my old one. I kept reminding myself it was only a week…

There was a football match the afternoon she left but I was in no mood for it. I just wanted to go home and listen to Chris Isaak for the week. As I arrived at the ground, my paranoia was already starting to flow. *Becky would forget all about me. She'd probably meet someone else over Christmas and never talk to me again.*

"We need to win this one, lads."

I glanced up to see John giving us a pep talk. His brother Lee was smoking his usual pre-match fag while a bleary-eyed Charlie was taking a swig of beer from a can. There were exactly eleven of us in the hut. No substitutes. Just a straight ninety minutes against one of the best teams in the league. They were called Spartak Red Machine for reasons no one had ever actually worked out, and chasing the Greyhound to win the league. They were also in the cup final and had three subs to call on.

"Billy, you with us?" Lee asked from beside John.

I nodded, my mind thinking of Becky.

A whole week without her.

"It'll be lonely this Christmas…" My inner jukebox started playing an old Mud song my dad had liked.

"Surprise," Becky's voice whispered from behind me.

I turned and nearly cried.

Becky, for her part, started to laugh. Jack joined in with a very cute giggle.

"Becky… Jack…" I stumbled, ignoring the shouts from the

others to get on the field.

"We were on our way to his nan's and then Jack started saying he wanted to see you play football. It's all I could get out of him. He had a massive tantrum and I thought, well, it might be fun…"

"They're waiting for you," Jack grinned, sounding way too grown-up for a five-year-old.

"I better go then," I smiled, not really wanting to leave Becky.

"Good luck," Becky said, pecking me on the cheek.

A few of the team started to wolf whistle. Something Jack seemed to find hilarious. I trotted on to the field and suddenly pretended to trip. I could hear Jack's laughter and started to grin the cheesiest grin of all time.

"See you've got yourself a fan club," John said, slapping me on the back.

"Yeah," I grinned, taking up my usual position as right back. With Becky and Jack watching, energy flowed through me. I was Pele. Hell, I was better than Pele.

"We're going to win," I told Charlie, who looked more than a little green.

He tried to smile but he was too hungover to do much more than stand in his position and not throw up.

I glanced over at Becky and Jack. Becky blew me a kiss and Jack waved. Becky looked gorgeous and Jack amazingly cute all wrapped up in a little red anorak with his Liverpool scarf around him. Becky started pointing furiously at something and it took me a few seconds to realise the game had actually started and their number seven was running towards me with the ball. He was fast. Very fast. Normally, he'd have passed with no problem.

But not with Becky and Jack watching. I slid into him and got the ball, sending it out to touch.

"Nice one," John said, slapping me on the back.

Ten minutes flew by. I was having an excellent game, running with far more speed and skill than I usually had. I was even yelling louder. Lee once suggested that the only reason I carried on playing football was because I liked the shouting. It had been a fair point. I was already feeling pretty chuffed with my game when, just before half-time, something strange happened.

I scored.

Now that might not sound strange, but it should. I'd never scored before. Ever. Even at school. Hell, half the time I used to miss when I was playing by myself in the back garden. It was a good goal as well. A bloody good goal. We'd been pressing them for a while, so Charlie and myself had moved up to the halfway line to watch. We'd have ventured further up front, but didn't want to get caught on the break. Mainly because we couldn't be arsed running all the way back. One of their defenders booted the ball upfield. It bounced about ten yards inside their half and I sprinted towards it, hoping to make contact before their attack did. I made it with yards to spare and wellied it back the way it came without any thought of control or skill. I glanced up to see the ball fly high over all our players, their defence and their surprised goalkeeper into the back of the net. For a few seconds, no one moved. Everyone just seemed to stare at the ball as it bounced against the net and slowly came to a stop.

"Goal!" I heard Jack's voice cry out from the side of the pitch. Everything started to move again. Their goalkeeper punched the air and cursed. My team ran towards me, yelling congratulations.

"Okay, lads," John said, "It was a fucking beautiful goal but let's not get carried away. There's still fifty minutes left. Billy, well done – but we still need you defending, okay?"

"No problem," I grinned back.

I fully intended to obey John's request, but a few minutes later we managed to get another corner. Spartak seemed to be a little shell-shocked by the goal and weren't playing as a team. We all knew that winning a game like this would be like winning the league. We'd be giant-killers. Other teams would look at us in a whole new light. I trotted up for the corner and hung around outside their penalty area, well away from the action and far enough back to make sure no one would get past me on a break. It wasn't something I'd normally do, but with Becky and Jack watching I wanted to look good. Lee took the corner. He always took the corners. Not only because he was good at them but also because he was the only one who could kick it all the way into the box. The ball floated above the whole defence and our attackers, moving toward the far post where no one was ever going to get it – no one but me. I read it perfectly and darted into the area, hurling myself at the ball and closing my eyes as it bounced off my head and into the net.

Two-nil the Cade!

Now that was something. Not only had I scored two goals but I'd managed to score more goals than we'd got in the last six games.

I was a sporting hero. Even the opposition were starting to look at me with respect.

Nothing much happened before half-time, but just after the break they pulled one back with a penalty when Charlie accidentally tripped one of their players up. It was such a stupid tackle even the referee seemed hard-pressed to send him off.

Lee moved back to defence in his place.

"Fucked if I'm going to let them get back in the game," he declared.

Down to ten men, we faced an onslaught. They were better than us when we had eleven men.

"We're the thin red line," John said, having a flashback to his army days as he pulled himself back to defend as well. "No one passes. No one."

Judging by the look in his eyes, I felt sorry for anyone who had the audacity to try.

I made a goal-line clearance and Lee nearly crippled their number five with a bone-crunching tackle that the ref, luckily, managed to completely miss.

Soon after, Lee had the ball in defence. Three of their players ran towards him, hoping he'd make a mistake.

"Lee, up the field," I yelled, spotting a hole in their defence.

Lee kicked it into the dead area behind their players. I shot forward, only to be butchered by their number eight, who swept me off the floor and into the air.

The world slowed. This was going to hurt, I thought, as I flew through the air, I'm like a human cannonball or…

Ouch.

The ref blew the whistle and Lee punched their number eight. It was a good punch and a much deserved one. The tackle could have easily broken both my legs and any another muscles that happened to be around. Some kind of fight had started as I struggled to my feet. John was pulling Lee away from the ref, who'd automatically pulled out a red card. He hadn't seen me recover so I had a quick relapse and started groaning in agony, amazed at the tackle hadn't left me feeling that bad.

"You okay?" the ref asked me, as I clutched my leg and groaned. It was a good show. I think I even managed to get a single tear out.

"Send him off!" I heard Jack shout from the side of the pitch.

I glanced up to see Jack yelling and crying at the ref. Becky didn't look too happy either.

I hobbled to my feet and waved heroically to Jack just as the ref was showing their number eight a red card. Or trying to. Two of his teammates were helping the semi-conscious player to his feet and off the field.

John slapped me on the back, causing more damage than the tackle had.

"We can still win this," he grinned.

Shortly after that they scored. It was a bloody good goal and, as we kicked off, all our heads were a little down.

Two-two.

We couldn't help feeling that things were getting back to normal. Any moment now, they'd score ten goals.

Only they didn't. Somehow we held on. It was the toughest, hardest twenty minutes any of us had ever played. I made another goal-line clearance, John a couple of terrifyingly hard but fair tackles. Becky and Jack kept up their support and I think their cheering not only inspired me but gave the whole team a buzz.

With only a few minutes to go, they were pressing us for the winning goal. We were on our last legs and near to collapse when the ball landed at my feet. I was on the edge of our own penalty area. Usually I'd have just belted it upfield, but this time I decided on a different approach and dribbled the ball to the touchline. A couple of their attackers followed me and slid in to get the ball. I somehow managed to get past them and glanced up – the way ahead was all clear. I started to run. Another player – their last defender – ran towards me and tried to break my legs. I leapt over the tackle. Suddenly I just had the goalkeeper to beat. He looked worried. Somewhere behind me, I heard my teammates roaring support and the opposition yelling abuse.

Everything was in slow motion. I knew I was going to score a hat-trick. As the goalkeeper rushed out to try and stop me, I whacked the ball past his outstretched body straight into…

…the post.

We both froze. The ball ricocheted to the edge of the six-yard box.

"Fuck!" I cursed, speeding towards it.

For one horrible moment, I thought the keeper would beat me.

But he didn't.

It was my day.

My toe touched the ball and it rolled slowly and beautifully over the line.

Three-two the Cade!

And the crowd went wild.

A few minutes after the restart, the ref blew the final whistle.

We'd won!

Becky and Jack came running onto the pitch. Becky gave me one of the best kisses of my life and Jack looked up at me as though I was the greatest footballer of all time.

As everyone left for the nearest pub, I loitered around Becky and Jack, seeing them off once again. All my doubts were gone. We'd make it. No question about it.

"I'm going to miss you," I said to her, after another goodbye kiss.

"I know," she smiled.

"Well?"

"Well what?"

"Well, aren't you going to miss me?"

"I might do…"

"Might do. Sheesh, you'd think after…"

"Easy tiger," she smiled. "I was just winding you up. Of course I'll miss you."

Jack was waving from the back of the car. I was trying to ignore the mist forming in my eyes.

As Becky got in, she wound the window down and kissed me again. Jack started to giggle in the back seat.

"I love you," she whispered, and then drove off.

This time, I didn't feel sad. Her parting words were echoing through my heart.

"I love you too," I whispered.

"Gee, thanks," John said, slapping me on the back. "Now let's get pissed!"

After a few beers, I wandered home, dancing on clouds and singing to myself. Wanting to share my good fortune with someone else, I stopped at Jimmy's. The rain had stopped, replaced by a rainbow, and I swear the rainbow was over Becky's house. I stared at it for a while, wishing she was still there, before knocking at Jimmy's.

"A rainbow," I said, as he opened the door.

"Wow," he smiled, no sarcasm present in his voice for the first time in years. We just stood there for a while looking at it. Jimmy was only wearing a towel, which seemed to amuse a few passers-by, but we didn't care. We both needed a rainbow and there one was. I glanced at Jimmy, who seemed more mellow and relaxed than he had done in ages. It was only when Gabriel joined us I understood why. They smiled at each other and it became pretty clear just why Jimmy was wearing a towel in the middle of the afternoon.

"Maybe you should put some clothes on," Gabriel suggested, with a bashfulness unbecoming to a tattooed skinhead. "People keep staring."

"Let them," Jimmy replied. "Rainbows don't last forever."

The three of us remained there, staring up at the sky. Not talking. Not needing to. Jimmy's hand slipped into Gabriel's. Mrs Peacock, a nosy stuck-up cow from number sixteen, walked by just in time to see Jimmy's towel fall off. She tried to look disgusted but found herself staring at his manhood for what seemed quite some time.

"Put your towel back on, James. You're scaring the neighbours," Gabriel smirked, adding, "Nice day for it, isn't it, dear?"

Mrs Peacock tutted her way home and the rainbow started to fade from view.

So we all went inside for a cup of tea.

Twelve

Happy, One Little Drink, Uh Oh

The next few days went by in a blur of phone conversations and Skyping. In between all the love-struck happiness, the film studies group finished filming "Day of the Trolleys" and moved on to the next project – a documentary about love. Christmas Day came and went with Mum refusing to take one sip of alcohol. For someone who spent the whole year drunk, it was kind of a habit that she wouldn't touch a drop at times the rest of the world was over-indulging. Although when I started to think about it, I hadn't seen her drinking much at all since my mugging.

And as the build-up to New Year started, only one thought was allowed in my head.

Becky.

The morning of New Year's Eve found me sitting in the garden with Happy playing the stick game. As a pup, he'd always enjoyed running after pretty much anything I threw, but had never quite got the idea of returning it. For Happy, the whole point of the game was to run after a stick and then try to get past me with it into his basket. If I ran towards him, he'd flash by trying to get inside. If he made it (and sometimes I'd let him) he'd come proudly walking back into the garden with a stupid grin on his face.

It was a good day. Cold but sunny. After about six or seven throws, I got bored of the stick game and decided to just sit down and think of Becky for a while. Happy wasn't impressed with this at first and kept looking up at me expectantly, before deciding to jump up and join me on the old stone chair in the garden.

My dad had built it just before Jenny died.

"Good boy," I whispered, patting Happy's head. "So, do you think this is it?" I asked.

I often asked Happy questions. I was convinced that dogs knew things the rest of us didn't. Mainly because they don't view time the way we do. They see everything that's happened and will happen. Ever wondered why, some nights when you're in the living room watching TV, your dog suddenly looks up at the door or runs around barking? That's because they're getting confused. They're seeing you in the future or you in the past and it's making their head hurt. Honest. It's true. That's why if I ever needed to know something important I'd ask Happy.

"So, is she the one?" I asked.

Happy started to lick my face enthusiastically.

I took that as a yes.

"Yeah, I think she is as well," I smiled. "It feels different from all the others. I feel like I've known her for years. That she's always been around."

"Woof," Happy replied.

"I can see myself with her," I explained.

Happy wanted me to explain. He was looking at me with his big doggy tongue hanging out. That was always a sure sign that he wanted me to explain something.

Or that he wanted some food.

"I don't mean just tonight either. I mean long-term. I can see us old and annoying the hell out of each other. You're a clever dog. I'm not used to this. What if she doesn't feel the same way? I thought Michelle loved me and she didn't even like me very much. There're women I've slept with I've not liked at all. What if Becky feels that way about me, what would I do then? I don't want to think about that. I…"

Happy leapt off and ran into some nearby bushes. I think I'd started to bore him.

Should I call her? I wanted to but I didn't want to sound desperate or anything. I'd talked to her the night before and we'd agreed to meet later that night, just before midnight, at her place. That was something to look forward to. I didn't want to blow my chances by pestering her and making her think I was some kind of arsehole. Christ, I needed a drink. It was a good ten hours before I'd get the chance to talk to her again. If I didn't do something to pass the time, I'd go stir crazy and make a fool out of myself the moment I saw her.

Just one little drink.

Never hurt anyone.

Seven hours later…

The Hope was spinning. That was odd. After all, I'd only had one little drink.

Just one little drink. Never hurt anyone. What time was it? What was time anyway and where was my whisky?

Whisky.

Whisky & Gin, whisky and gin, Rebecca Swan drinks whisky and gin.

I'm not drunk. No way. Ah, there's my whisky.

"Fucking good game last week," Charlie said. "Your third goal was fucking mag... mag... brilliant."

Someone was talking to me. I could tell 'cause of the words and stuff. I looked around and saw Charlie standing there, grinning and handing me another drink.

He looked well pissed.

"The thing is with Becky... I mean, I know that it's all... What time is it?"

"Eight."

"Fuck."

"Yeah."

I finished my Scotch and looked around the bar. It was already full of people starting to celebrate the New Year. Life was good. Everything was good and going right.

"I'm seeing her tonight, you know. She's coming back esp... especially for me. That's good, that is. That means she likes me."

"Listen, Billy," John said from behind the bar. "You know it goes against my religion to say this, but don't you think you've had enough? At the rate you're going you'll be unable to remember her name by midnight, let alone welcome her back."

"Rubbish," I replied. "I've only had one little drink."

I tried to place my glass back on the bar, only to find someone had moved the bar from under me. The glass went smashing to the ground. It was all very confusing. I just stared at my empty hand, trying to work out what had happened to my drink.

"Christ, you're pissed," Mad Tommy said from his usual place at the bar.

"Oops." I looked up at John and swayed steadily back and forth. "I think I will nip home. Just to freshen up before… I'm not drunk or anything like that."

"Course you're not," John said, shaking his head. "Charlie, could you give him a hand?"

The rest was a little bit of a blur. Mad Tommy decided to help me as well, finding my drunken state exceedingly funny. I was starting to worry. When Mad Tommy laughed because you were drunk, that was serious. Charlie lived just around the corner from mine and as we reached his house, lightning cut open the sky and the heavens opened.

"Want a coffee?" he asked. "Until the rain stops, like?"

Somehow, I was sitting on a couch. I had no memory at all of getting from the door to the couch. Part of my head was saying I should be at home or waiting for Becky or anywhere but Charlie's, sitting on his twenty-year-old stained sofa.

Thunder bellowed again as Charlie offered me a mug of coffee.

For a moment, he looked like Vincent Price in an old horror film.

"Cheers," I said.

Coffee would work. Sober me up.

"No offence, Charlie, but this coffee tastes a bit weird," I said, handing him the empty mug back.

"Put some whisky in it, just for taste," Charlie grinned.

"Charles?" a woman's voice cried out. "Is that you?"

The voice was a little slurred, but I recognised it as belonging to Lil, Charlie's wife and a woman who, not to put too fine a point on it, had been described as mad as a hatter by just about everyone. Including several people who genuinely were mad as hatters. It suddenly dawned on me why I never used to go to Charlie's.

1. I hated Lil with a passion.

2. I wasn't that mad about Charlie.

Mad Tommy had already nodded off, curled up in a foetal position while suckling a bottle of Newcastle Brown Ale.

"Got any more coffee?" I asked.

Charlie winked and handed me another mug.

Becky.

She was probably on her way home now. It'd be good to see her. I should get home, get ready. Just finish this coffee…

I had a weird dream. There was this clown with a baseball bat. He was laughing hysterically and lifting the bat back for a big swing. I woke sweating only to find myself in bed with Becky on top of me. I had no memory at all of how I'd ended up in bed or why I still had all my clothes on. The lights were out and I could just see her silhouette as she undressed. I moved my head back to the pillow and wondered what the strange smell was. Like old socks mixed with rotting and overcooked cabbage. I looked up to see Becky's silhouette again. I couldn't help thinking she'd had a busy Christmas as she'd put on quite a bit of weight, and who was that snoring in the background and mumbling to himself in his sleep? It sounded like Mad Tommy but it couldn't be because he must've still been at Charlie's and it wasn't Becky crawling on top of me naked – it was Lil!!

"Er, what do you think you're doing?" I asked, suddenly very much awake and very much sober.

"Seducing you," she slurred. "You can kiss me if you want to."

"I'd rather not," I replied, trying to be polite about it while ignoring the rising tide of panic. I started to worm my way out from under her but, before I could get far, Charlie flicked on the light and the whole world went to hell in a handbasket.

"What the fuck do you think you're doing?" he yelled.

"Nothing!" I cried, pushing her off.

The noise had woken Mad Tommy and he staggered into the bedroom like some weird and terrifying Frankenstein's monster.

"So that's where she put you," he grinned. "I was wondering why she was helping you to bed. Out like a light you was."

Lil was stark naked, Charlie dressed only in some tatty Y-fronts that had once been white, a long time ago. The whole scene did not look good.

"I wasn't talking to you, Billy. I was talking to that bitch," Charlie yelled.

"I didn't mean to, I just…" Lil started to say, bursting into tears.

"Every time I bring a mate back you have to try to fuck 'em. What is with you?"

"I don't fuck them, Charlie. Well, only Jesse and that was years ago!"

"He was my fucking best man, you bitch. We'd just got bloody married! I should've known then. We're through."

I'd never seen Charlie so angry. He vanished for a moment and then I heard a door slam. Lil followed him straight out.

"Heh heh heh," Tommy cackled. "She's still naked."

As soon as he finished, he doubled up and started to vomit. When he'd stopped, he bent over, pulled his false teeth from the puke and put them straight back in his mouth.

"Say, what are you doing here anyway? I thought you were meeting that Becky girl?"

FUCK!

I looked at the clock. It was ten to twelve.

Becky!!

I could still make it.

I rushed straight out of the house, almost colliding with Lil and Charlie.

They were standing in the road, blocking my way out and having the slanging match to end all slanging matches.

"It wasn't me!" Lil yelled, with a scream loud enough to wake the dead and any neighbours. "It was Billy, he seduced me!"

"Fuck off!" Charlie replied.

"Yeah, fuck off!" I added.

"But Charles, I love you. I do. Please, Charles, give me another chance."

"One more word and I'll fucking kill you!"

Okay, a little bit of my brain said, murder's bad. Everyone knows that – and letting someone murder someone is also bad. They told you that at school. Any self-respecting human being would try and stop them.

"Er, Charlie…" I started to say as I approached the couple.

For a second, Lil stopped crying and they both looked at me.

"Could I get past, please?"

For a while the three of us just stood there, like the three cowboys at the end of *The Good, the Bad and the Ugly*. I was the Good, but it was a toss-up between Charlie and Lil who was the Bad and who was the Ugly.

"You think I'd want to fuck Billy?" Lil screamed, breaking the silence. "I mean look at him!"

Charlie did just that and I started to feel myself getting more than a little annoyed.

"I don't. I'd much rather have you," she continued, dropping to her knees and begging him to take her back.

I seized my chance and hopped over her. It was tricky but just manageable.

"I love you, Charlie. I really do," she sobbed. "But you don't make it easy for me. That's why I do things like I do. I don't even like Billy."

I was almost home free and had actually reached the bottom of my road when Lil rushed up and grabbed my arm.

"William," Lil cried, throwing herself at me. "You want me, don't you? Tell him how good I am. Tell him."

"Lil, what the fuck do…?"

The words froze in my mouth as I caught sight of Becky's car pulling into her drive. I guess she was running late as well. I looked down and saw the still-naked Lil clinging to me, sobbing.

All things considered, it probably didn't look good. Becky got out of the car and came marching over.

"What's going on?" she asked, her voice managing to sound nervous and angry at the same time.

My mouth opened, but before words could come out Charlie spouted bullshit.

"I caught him shagging my bird, didn't I? You'd be better off without him if you ask me."

Fear shot through me. A cold fear that was intensified by the look of betrayal in Becky's eyes.

"I didn't…" I started to say, but by then Becky had turned and started to run to her flat.

"Come on, admit it," Lil coughed, specks of phlegm shooting from her mouth. "Tonight meant something to you, didn't it?"

Somewhere, a clock started to strike midnight.

Lil moved in to kiss me.

Bells started ringing.

"Get the fuck off me!" I yelled, trying to gently push her away.

The baseball bat hit home.

It was a gentle push, but Lil was still seven shades to the wind and staggered back, tripping off the edge of the pavement, into the road and a waiting puddle.

I looked up to see Becky turning her head and catching sight of Lil falling backwards. It looked like I'd punched her.

Becky dropped her keys.

"Becky!" I shouted, trying to run across the road to catch her – only to be grabbed by Charlie.

Becky rushed inside, slamming the door behind her.

"You leave my Lil alone!" Charlie roared, taking a wild swing at me.

Distracted by Becky, Charlie's punch hit home and knocked me over. I pushed myself up and started to move towards Becky's. Hoping that it wasn't too late to fix things.

"Hit him again, Charlie. He's a cunt!" Lil screamed.

A few people were starting to come out of the houses now to witness my latest moment of glory.

My mood was getting worse.

Charlie took another mad swing at me. The first punch I'd not registered. Charlie punched like a girl and I'd been more concerned with reaching Becky. When the second one struck, the reality of it all hit home and I started to feel pissed off. The next few seconds were a blank. It took four people to drag me off Charlie. By the time they did, his nose was bleeding, and Lil was screaming and calling me several very inventive names, none of which were very nice.

"Should I call the cops, love?" one of the blokes holding me asked. I think it was Ken from number twenty-two. I considered hitting him as well but then thought better of it. He wasn't a bad bloke and was only trying to stop me killing Charlie.

"It's all right. I'm cool now," I lied.

"Fuck off!" Lil shouted. "Get the cops, Charlie, he attacked me. You saw him!"

"Listen, this is fucked. I'm calling the police, let them sort it all out," Ken said.

Quite a few lights were on in the street now. People would be talking about this for days. Mr Jones had his mobile out again to record it all.

"You want the police here?" I asked Charlie, staring him out. "That'll give John and Lee a right laugh. You know how we're mates. Probably put us a player down at the weekend too when they see your console collection."

The penny started to slowly drop. He had three options. He could fuck off, call the police and get arrested, or have Lee and John asking after him.

Getting a few punches from Billy Cade was one thing, but having the Wayne brothers looking for you was something else.

"Charles, what's up?" Lil asked, as observant as ever.

"Nothing," Charlie replied, staring at his feet, the clouds or anywhere other than at me.

"Charlie, where you going? Aren't you going to sort him out? He's asking for it," Lil said, preparing for a role as a UN peacekeeper.

"Shut up and get in the house," he snapped, wiping the blood away from his nose.

"Don't tell me to shut up!" Lil answered, catching him up and slapping him on the back and head.

Everyone gathered around could hear them argue all the way down the path and even after their front door slammed. The neighbours huffed almost as one and started to wander off.

It started to rain. I didn't bother moving.

There didn't seem much point. The lights were on in Becky's house but the curtains were drawn. She was probably putting Jack to bed about now. I looked up at Jimmy's house but the lights were off. He was off gigging somewhere. Without warning, I found myself outside Becky's, ringing the doorbell. When that didn't work, I decided on a less subtle approach and started to bang my fist against the door yelling her name out like some pot-bellied Northern Romeo.

The door eventually opened, the safety chain still on.

"I thought you were different," she said.

My heart cracked.

"I didn't… it wasn't…"

My words were shabby and pathetic.

She closed the door without saying a word.

I stared at it for a while hoping reality would change.

A dark sense of unreality crept over me.

This wasn't happening.

This couldn't be happening.

The version of myself that had planned to spend the rest of his life with Becky shrivelled up and died.

Somewhere behind me a clown was laughing, and in his hands was a fucking big baseball bat.

There was no sleep. The night was spent staring at the ceiling, hoping it was all some kind of weird fucking dream. Dawn found me in the back garden, standing on the patio watching the rain. I don't think it had stopped all night. Happy decided to join me, even though he was still half asleep. Time blurred until I heard my mum's voice calling me inside for breakfast.

Breakfast was a sullen affair. She didn't say much, but I could tell she'd heard and thought the worst. Probably like everyone else. I was about to go to Becky's when I saw her running into Jimmy's.

"It's not a good time right now," he said, looking a little awkward.

"Listen, I know Becky's here. I just wanted to explain everything. I know it looked bad, but it wasn't. It was just… it was just a stupid fucking mistake."

"A naked woman was all over you in the middle of the street, her boyfriend was ready to belt you because you'd fucked her, and you say it was nothing!?" Becky suddenly yelled from Jimmy's side. She'd been crying, but the tears had now been replaced by rage and betrayal.

I thought back to the story of her dead husband and how he'd been seeing someone else. After something like that, I guessed you must expect the worst.

"Nothing happened," I replied, starting to realise just how

useless my case was.

"I trusted you," she whispered.

My mouth opened, but Becky turned away before I could reply.

"I didn't do anything, Jimmy. You've got to believe me," I said.

There was doubt in Jimmy's eyes.

"She didn't need last night," he said, closing the door.

I looked down at my hands. They were shaking. A thin mist seemed to be settling over everything. I staggered home like a ghost, closed the door and slumped against the wall, my insides vanishing.

I'd blown it with Becky.

Happy New Year.

Thirteen

Aftermath

It was all fucked.

Fourteen

Black Friday, Chris Isaak and the Pit

If life was fair I could have talked to Becky and explained things. She'd have believed me and we'd have had a passionate make-up session. Life's not like that though. I tried to talk to her too many times to count, but she didn't want to see me. As miserable as I was, hope refused to leave my side. For most of the month I remained convinced things would work out. We were meant to be together. Nothing could stop that. The music I was listening to didn't help. Lots of Chris Isaak and Jeff Buckley. I made a few old-school playlists for Becky via Spotify. No joy. I tried to find Charlie and Lil, so they could set the record straight, but they'd vanished. Apparently John and Lee had expressed an interest in having a quiet chat with them about what had really happened on New Year's Eve. They'd panicked and left town, while Mad Tommy couldn't remember a thing.

I was miserable, but part of me was revelling in it. I still loved Becky, and the fact that she was still mad at me meant there was still emotion present. Okay, so the emotions were hate, loathing and a desire to kill, but it was better than nothing.

That all changed on Black Friday. The day I was forced to accept reality. I was at Jimmy's when the phone rang. We'd made a peace of sorts a week or so after it had happened – mainly thanks to Gabriel's intervention – but things were still a little awkward between us. I answered, only to find Becky on the other end. When she heard me say hello I could almost sense the ice on the line.

"How's things?" I asked.

Sometimes we need to say things that just can't be said.

"Fine," she whispered, falling silent for a while. Her voice suddenly seemed like a stranger's. Shards of ice lanced my heart. Something was coming. Something bad. A juggernaut. I knew what I had to say just as much as I knew her answer would be the juggernaut hitting me.

"I love you," I whispered, closing my eyes and praying for miracles.

You should never tell someone you love them over the phone. There should be fireworks, explosions, rain and neon, or at the very least a chance in hell.

"I know," Becky answered, no emotion present.

God pressed pause on my life, and for a moment everything was possible and I knew she really did love me and was just having a little trouble admitting it. Everything was going to be cool between us forever and ever and ever and…

"I don't love you."

"Oh."

"Tell Jimmy I'll call later," she continued, as though her words hadn't killed me.

"Sure," I somehow managed to answer, staying on the line for a moment, but no words passed between us. I looked down and saw my own body lying there, dead and dusted.

The line fell silent as she put the phone down.

"No, you don't understand," I continued. "I love you."

"Billy…" Jimmy whispered from somewhere far behind me.

His presence hardly registered. The only things I was aware of were Becky's words and a total sense of unreality.

"I know. I don't love you."

It just wasn't possible. I'd been so sure, so certain that she was the one. Even through all the shite, most of me had thought it was just a hiccup, something we'd laugh about when we were eighty and telling our great-grandchildren about how we met.

"I don't love you."

And what did I say?

"Oh."

Not "I love you more than anything that's ever existed and life without you has no meaning."

Not "Please, I need you. I think you need me. We're meant to be together, can't you tell?"

Just "Oh."

"Billy…"

There was a mug of tea in my hands. Jimmy was pushing me back into a chair.

"She doesn't love me," I said, looking up at him and wishing more than anything I could cry.

Maybe tears would've made the pain go away. And it was just the start. I was too numb to feel any real pain. That would follow.

"I know," Jimmy whispered. "I'm sorry."

It was hard to breathe. My hands were shaking. It was all useless and fucked. There was no point to it.

No point to any fucking thing at all.

"I don't love you."

Why had it gone wrong?

Had there been anything wrong before New Year's Eve?

"I love her," I stated, looking at Jimmy.

"I know. I don't know what to say."

"There's nothing to say," I replied, placing the mug on a coffee table. "I thought she was the one. I really did."

More silence. I needed to go home. I needed to be home in my bedroom more than anything else in the whole fucking world.

"I've got to go," I said, rising to my feet.

"It'll get better," Jimmy said, not really meaning it. "And you know if you need to talk about it…"

"Thanks. I just need some time to myself. I just… I'll see you later."

I walked home oblivious to everything. I caught sight of Becky looking down at me from the window of her place. For an instant I saw us both there only a few weeks before, looking down at the street and then kissing.

I looked back up at her window and it was empty.

"I don't love you."

Once inside I climbed the stairs to my room and shut the door, slumped behind it and closed my eyes.

"I don't love you."

Part of me was missing.

Becky was gone. It had been nearly a month. I should've known. I should've...

The simple truth was that there was nothing there. She didn't love me.

I looked at the bottle of Jack on my dressing table. An early Christmas present from Becky. Why the fuck did I drink that day? What was it about this town... my life... that made me drink so much?

What the fuck was wrong with me?

It didn't matter. Only one thing mattered.

Becky didn't love me.

And that's all there was to it.

Fifteen

Punches, Parties and Passion

"Love. Is it worth all the hassle or just a big pile of shite?" I asked.

We were in the Lamb, starting our next project for the video course – a documentary about love.

"Cut," Kate said, shaking her head.

The documentary had been my idea and seemed a good one back when I was in love. Here and now it seemed a complete waste of time and a painful reminder of everything I'd lost. I was already drunk, and in a foul mood. I hadn't been a happy drunk all year. Or a happy anything come to think of it. The snow was falling outside – winter had hit the town hard even though people kept telling me spring was just around the corner. Somehow it all made sense. I'd not talked to Becky since that day on the phone – more than four weeks before. The pain hadn't got any better. It was still there, gnawing away at my insides. Just when I thought things couldn't get worse, Jimmy had let slip

Becky had started seeing Jez again. I wasn't at my best.

"Billy," Kate urged.

"What?" I asked, trying to appear innocent.

John shook his head.

"Can't you just read what we talked about?" Kate asked.

"But it's all so pointless, isn't it" I answered.

"Okay, we'll do the opening later," Kate sighed. "For now, let's start some of the interviews. We can splice them together later. That couple over there seem happy. Let's start with them."

Kate pointed me towards the corner of the pub where a young couple were holding hands over the table. Kate was right. They were not only young and good-looking, but hopelessly and blissfully in love.

I hated them instantly.

"Hi," I said, approaching their table. "We're doing a documentary about love and couldn't help noticing you two. Do you mind if I just ask you a few questions?"

"Could we have a copy?" the girl asked. "Only it's our anniversary today and it'd be great to have something to remember it by."

"No problem," Kate said from behind me. "Could you just stand near Billy, he's the happy-looking man with the mike? That's great. Right. Take one."

Kate didn't need to say take one. Everything was take one. But it made her feel better so we always let it go.

"So it's your anniversary," I said to the couple, putting on my best fake smile. "How long have you been seeing each other?"

"Two months today," the boy grinned.

"We met at midnight on New Year's Eve. Isn't that romantic?"

"Billy…" Kate whispered.

"Are you okay?" the girl asked.

"Sure," I smiled, looking a lot like the Joker from the *Batman* comic. "Sorry, do you mind telling us your names?"

"Sure. This is William and I'm Rebecca."

Somewhere Life started to laugh.

"They're good names," I replied, holding back any emotion. "What makes you think you two will last, though?"

"We love each other," they both said, holding hands tightly and looking really bloody annoying.

"I know, but love's just a chemical reaction, isn't it? Did you know that scientists recently proved it lasts eighteen months, if that? What will you do then, when you stop loving each other and realise the truth?"

"We'll never stop loving…" the girl tried to say, but by then I was on a roll.

"I mean, one of you will fuck around and if you don't the other one will probably think you have and dump you anyway. Then one of you will start going out with the person the other one hates more than anyone else in the world and one of you will find themselves in a black pit of despair from which there's no escape, catch cancer and die."

The girl started to cry. The boy hit me. The lights went out.

"Well, you had it coming," Gabriel said later.

After regaining my senses and receiving various lectures from Kate, I'd sought shelter at Jimmy's. At first, they'd both been concerned. Unfortunately, any concern had promptly vanished when I told them how it happened.

"In fact, you're lucky the guy only punched you once."

"I hate to say this, but you've really got to deal with it. You've changed over the last few weeks. Everyone's noticed it."

I remained silent.

"I've got an idea," Gabriel said. "Something that could help lift your spirits."

I was starting to think going to Jimmy's had been a bad idea. For friends, they weren't showing much concern for my latest bit of bad luck. They'd even laughed when I'd told them Kate was keen on keeping my latest indiscretion in the documentary.

"Nothing could lift my spirits," I said glumly. "Unless Becky's changed her mind about me."

"'Fraid not," Gabriel said. "But you're welcome to this if you want."

He pulled out a ticket and waved it in front of my face.

"Anfield next Saturday. Man United."

"I guess it'd help," I said, secretly ecstatic but trying to maintain my miserable-as-sin pose.

"Oh well, if you're not bothered, I'll use it myself. I just thought it might cheer you up."

"No, it would. Sorry, I'm just still not with it. Maybe it's about time to get out there again – and Anfield's a good place to start."

"Okay," he said, handing me the ticket. "As long as you promise to enjoy yourself."

"I'll try," I said, smiling for the first time that year. "But how did you get it?"

"I used to know someone in the team," he winked. "But let's

not press that one. Just take it and enjoy."

I'd not been to Anfield for a long time and it felt good. On the bus to the ground, I found myself thinking about Becky, but as soon as I joined the crowd marching into the stadium, she started to slip to the back of my mind and, for the first time since Black Friday, I started to live the now. If you're not a football fan, you're missing out on one of life's truly great experiences. Liverpool were not having a good season. United were top, Liverpool mid table with no chance of winning anything. The game started badly. One of their players fell over some grass outside the Liverpool penalty area and got a free kick. They scored. The crowd were not amused.

Fucking great, I thought. *Typical of my luck.*

I became convinced that it wasn't Liverpool's fault they were losing, but mine. My life was so bad that it was starting to affect those around me. Liverpool were going through a bad streak because I was going though a bad streak.

We were both going to get relegated.

Then we scored. The crowd went wild. There's no ground like Anfield for loud, over-the-top support and nothing like a goal against their main rivals to get the crowd going. For the next eighty minutes there was nothing else in my life other than the match. It was Zen. It felt like I'd always been there and always would be there. If Liverpool won, all would be well with the world. If United won, I was doomed. I didn't know what form the doom would take, I just knew I would be doomed. I wasn't sure what would happen if it was a draw. United scored again, but before we could all get depressed Liverpool equalised. At half-time, I just slumped in the plastic seat and took in the whole thing. It was cool. Life was cool. So Becky didn't love me. It was time for me to grow up, get a life and realise that things didn't always work out the way they should. I thought back to when I was very, very young and Man United beat Liverpool two-one. My response was brave for one so small – I went straight into the front garden and started to replay the game all by myself. The score was twenty-six-nil to Liverpool (all goals scored by Cade, their amazing new striker) when my dad came home from work and tried to sympathise.

"Never mind, I'm sure they'll win next time," he said, ruffling my hair.

He might've been trying to say the right thing, but his words brought the full horror of the result back to me and I burst out crying and ran inside. My mum found out what was happening and shouted at my dad, who still wasn't sure what he'd done. But now it was two-all at half-time and I just knew Liverpool were going to win.

The next forty-five minutes were the longest and best I'd endured since Black Friday. It was an amazing game and, if it had been anyone other than United, I'd probably have admitted that both sides played a brilliant game. But I was still more than happy when Liverpool scored the winner seconds before the final whistle.

They say the roar coming from the Kop was heard in Australia. I believe it. My own cry was so loud that my voice was fucked for the rest of the night. I turned around and hugged some fat bloke to my right. Tears were streaming down his bright red face. Football games are one of the few occasions where it's possible for heterosexual Northern blokes to hug. We'd done it. Something had gone right.

The world was mine and, for a while, everything seemed possible.

I guess that's how I ended up sleeping with Michelle.

It happened like this.

I got back home about ten and decided to celebrate Liverpool's victory down the Hope. A few Man United fans drank there and I wanted to laugh at them. Needless to say booze was consumed. Someone, I can't remember who, said some guy I knew from the team was having a party and had invited Becky. In my drunken high, I knew this would be a great day to get back together with her. I couldn't think of anything better. Liverpool beat Manchester United and I fix things with Becky and live happily ever after. I found myself at the house around midnight with half a bottle of Jack in hand. The other half was already doing a Charleston in my bloodstream. Judging by the crowd, it wasn't a bad do. One of those all-but-mythical decent house parties you find on occasion. I did an instant sweep of the guests and froze when I saw Becky on the floor talking to some friends. I tried to smile but wasn't sure if I'd managed to before she turned away. The J.D. bottle went straight to my lips.

"Whatever you do, don't turn around," Chrissie said.

Obviously, this meant I had to turn around and straight away I wished I hadn't. Charlie and Lil had just come in, Lil already a little the worse for wear and Charlie very nervous. I contemplated beating the shit out of him. Or at least pounding his head into the floor until he decided to tell the truth about Black Friday. I glanced down at the J.D. bottle, only to find it was empty. I still wasn't remotely drunk but could feel anger trying to push its way to the surface.

"You want me to take him outside and kick the shit out of him?" Lee asked.

I considered the possibility for a while and, I've got to admit, it was appealing, but decided against it. Hell, Liverpool had won. What had happened had happened.

"Forget it," I said, turning my attention back to Becky.

The rest of the night was spent with me wandering around the party trying, and failing, not to stare at Becky. She didn't look my way once.

"I miss Becky," I said to just about everyone at the party, including the cat. "I really thought she was the one for me."

At one point, I wandered into the kitchen to find a couple of Lee's old army mates standing by the bottles, smoking fags. I pushed through them and grabbed a bottle of whisky from the sink. Lee and Chrissie came in for a while and we started mindless party chatter. Somehow I managed to turn this around to a ramble about Becky. It was getting to be a theme of the evening.

"I mean, I don't know what else I can do," I said, failing to notice the people gradually leaving until only Chrissie and a slightly embarrassed Lee were left.

"It'll be all right," Chrissie smiled.

Lee stared at the ceiling.

"Liverpool did well today, didn't they?" he said, hoping to get the conversation away from emotions to something he felt more at home with. Chrissie gave him a look.

"What?" he replied, with a shrug of his shoulders.

"William is having a really bad night and all you can do is talk about football. I thought you were supposed to be his friend."

"Well, it's stupid," Lee said.

I felt an argument rising, but not from me. I also felt more than a little invisible.

"He's been moping around for weeks. If he really loved Becky, he'd do something to get her back."

"What can I do?" my voice said weakly.

"What can he do?" Chrissie said. "He's tried to explain. I think it's really sad. What if she was the one for him? How do you think he feels being at this party knowing she's in the other room – probably getting off with a new boyfriend."

"Pretty awful," I said. "I mean, it's like… What new boyfriend?"

"Well, if he had any balls," Lee interrupted, "he'd go in there and show her that he was enjoying himself. There's nothing a woman hates more than seeing someone she's dumped have a good time!"

I thought Chrissie was going to yell back but she didn't.

"He's got a point," she said, dragging Lee into the garden for a cig, leaving me alone in the kitchen.

I could hear the music and chat from just beyond the kitchen door. I looked at my reflection in the darkness of the window and allowed myself a moment's depression. Becky was never going to be mine. I had to admit that and just get on with my life. Maybe there was no love anywhere and we were all doomed.

Still, at least Liverpool had won.

It was then I heard her voice behind me.

Lil.

A drunk Lil.

"Hi," she slurred, looking everywhere but at me for a while. "What have you done with your voice?"

"Sorry?" I replied, not realising my voice was still a little hoarse from all the shouting at the football match.

"I just wanted to apologise for New Year's Eve," she said. "I was very, very drunk. I didn't know what I was doing."

"Yeah," I replied, trying and failing to get past her.

"If there's anything I can do to help, just let me know."

For a second, I thought I was hearing things.

"Well, you could tell Becky the truth," I suggested.

"What do you mean?" she said, sipping wine from the bottle she was holding.

"You know, the truth," I repeated.

"I guess so. But what is the truth anyway?" she said, still not allowing me an escape from the kitchen.

"I mean, if I told the whole truth it would shatter Charles. He's secretly quite pleased that he saved me from you."

"He didn't save…"

"And if I really told the truth… I've not been exactly faithful over the years, you know."

Of course I knew. It was common knowledge. Anyone who'd read the graffiti in the Hope toilet knew. Lil's reputation was said to have reached wise men sitting alone on mountains in Tibet.

"I've slept with lots of men Charles doesn't know about," she said, moving closer to me. "Sometimes when he's been right in the next room. Like that night we had together. Doesn't it get you… excited?"

A number of snappy comebacks shot through my head. I needed something that wasn't going to cause too much trouble but would also make her get the message.

"You jumped on me when I was comatose and then told everyone I'd tried to shag you," I said. "What the fuck…?"

"Yeah, but it was fun, wasn't it?" she said, trying and failing to look sexy.

"You've ruined my fucking life," I snapped, pushing her hand from my belt.

The words were like a slap. Momentarily stunned, she didn't move. I seized my chance for freedom and rushed past her out of the kitchen and into the relative safety of the hall. I was just about to stagger into the living room when I caught sight of Michelle.

"Listen, you've got to help me," I said. "Lil's coming on to me again. Is it alright if we just talk for a minute until she gets the message that I'm not interested?"

"What have you done to your voice?" Michelle asked, sliding closer. "It sounds dead sexy."

"Really?"

"Yeah."

"Thanks. Hey, congratulations on the engagement." I was surprised to find that I actually meant it. Despite everything that had happened, there was still a little soft spot for Michelle lurking somewhere in my cesspool of a mind.

"Didn't you hear? It's all off." She looked down at her drink. "He wasn't the one for me."

"William, could you get me a drink, please?" Lil said from nearby.

Her bad breath made both me and Michelle flinch.

"Do you mind? He's with me," Michelle answered, placing an arm protectively around me.

"You…" Lil started to say and then almost fell over, steadying herself against the wall.

"Are you alright, love?" one of Lee's army mates said, helping her to remain upright.

"I don't think…" I started to say, only to be stopped by Michelle.

"He'll find out," she whispered, placing her other arm over my shoulder. "I'm very drunk, you know. If you wanted to, you could probably take advantage of me."

Before I knew what was happening, I was being kissed and I've got to admit, as experiences go, it wasn't a bad one.

Now you might well think that this was very shallow behaviour on my part. After all, I had spent the last two months moaning about the loss of Becky, only going to the party in the sincere hope of winning her back. There was no doubt in my mind that Becky was the one, the only one, for me. On the other hand, I had drunk more than a bottle of bourbon and was suddenly feeling very horny and had fancied Michelle since, well, since whenever.

The next hour or so was spent in one long snogging session. While we were kissing, a number of things were happening around us that we were both totally oblivious to. Becky left the party alone. Lee and Chrissie left shortly after, Lee slapping me on my back and shouting, "Good one, lad. Get in there!" before an icy look from Chrissie silenced him.

A couple of fights started. One of which somehow landed in the middle of Michelle and me, splitting the two of us up for a moment. Fortunately, the two men rolled away to carry their fight into the lounge. We decided we'd be safer in the now empty kitchen and proceeded to get even more intimate, knocking several empty bottles on the floor and scaring the cat. Meanwhile, Lil's soldier had found out just what she was like. Lil'd used what little charm she had on him and he'd soon found himself on a couch with his hand up her dress. According to the few witnesses still at the party, it was at this point Charlie returned to the house from the back garden, where he'd been smoking blow. His reaction was simple and straightforward. He walked up to the soldier and hit him over the head with a vase. A couple of the bloke's pals were about to kill Charlie before it became clear that Lil was his wife, at which point they all called her a few interesting names and apologised to Charlie, who stormed out alone. A crying but fully clothed Lil followed him.

All in all it was a pretty good party.

Back in the kitchen, any form of language had been replaced by grunts as we smashed against the cooker. We also rolled around on the sink, the washer, the table and under the table before finishing, so to speak, against the kitchen door.

"Hi," I said, afterwards, still breathing heavily.

"Hi," Michelle smiled, kissing me again.

We were about to start the whole sordid and exceptionally pleasant procedure again when Mad Tommy started to snore in the living room.

"Let's go to my place," she smiled, leading me out of the house.

We crashed into Michelle's and I couldn't help smiling as we passed the door. For an instant, I saw myself there throwing up a few months before. A bad night. This one was better.

The whole thing was enough to make me believe in God. Almost.

Sixteen

Sex, Tristesse and Revelations

I awoke in the middle of the night, my arm wrapped around Michelle, her naked body close to mine. I could feel her heat. It was part of me. For a while I was happy. Content. I was with Michelle.

Michelle.

I could see myself standing by the side of the bed, taking a bow and pointing to any ghosts who happened to be passing through.

'Look, look who I've just made love to!' my ghost-self kept saying to anyone willing to listen. 'Michelle. *The* Michelle. After all these years, the kid's finally gone and done it. Nice one.'

I allowed myself a smile. Maybe this was what success felt like. Maybe this was it. Maybe this was…

Becky.

The name came from nowhere and everywhere without my permission.

Becky who? I tried to tell myself, already feeling the guilt starting to rise like a dark tide inside my soul. Or what passed for my soul.

I was with Michelle. I should live the now. She felt great. She really did.

Becky. The voice in my head repeated.

I never liked Becky, I told the voice.

You did so like her. I was there.

No, honest. I was just on the rebound from Michelle. She was the one I really wanted.

So why do you wish Becky was lying next to you instead of Michelle?

I do not.

Come off it, this is yourself you're talking to. You can't lie to me.

I can. I've lied to you for years. It's the only way to get through the day.

Okay, so you can lie to me, but you know you're lying and it makes you feel really guilty. Take Michelle. What if she loves you? How are you going to tell her that you don't love her?

But I do.

No you don't. You're not even sure you like her that much.

How can I not love her? She's beautiful.

Well, for a start, she used to go out with Geoff and you hate him. Do you really think you're going to like someone who's spent a great deal of her recent time liking him? Not to mention shagging him. You've had sex with the same woman he has. He was probably better than you as well.

Shut up and anyway, I do love her. Honest.

Don't.

Do.

Don't.

Do.

Becky.

Oh, shut up.

I can't shut up. I'm you. And don't talk to me like that. Becky's the one you love and you blew it with her and said you wouldn't sleep with anyone you don't have feelings for and what do you go and do? You sleep with the first woman you get the chance to sleep with.

I'm a bloke, that's what we do!

You're a prick. A sad, selfish prick. Becky was right, at least Bullion and his cronies are honest about what they are, but not you. You like to think you're so special, but you're not. You're worse than any of them and you've probably got her pregnant.

I'm not worse than any of them and… what do you mean, pregnant?

Let's put it this way, I don't see any condoms around.

I don't have any on me. It's bad luck. I never get laid if I take condoms to a party, and I didn't know I was going to go to a party anyway.

It's bad luck to get someone like Michelle up the duff. She doesn't love you.

She won't be pregnant.

Your Uncle Danny got your auntie pregnant after just the one time – and he used a condom.

She won't be pregnant.

How do you know?

I just do.

Well, that's comforting. We'll both have to pay maintenance you know. What if she's already pregnant and just fucking you to make you think that you got her pregnant and marry her so she can sponge off you for the rest of your life, making each and every day a living, impoverished hell?

Are you sure you're my subconscious?

Yeah, why?

Well, recently every day has been a living and impoverished hell so having a kid would make a nice change.

But you don't want to become a dad yet, at least not with Michelle.

And what's that supposed to mean?

Becky.

Oh shut up. I mean it. Just shut the fuck up.

Becky. Becky. Becky. Becky. Becky. Beautiful Becky. She really loved you as well. You could have lived happily ever after with her, but you had to go and blow it.

My arm's dead.

Stop trying to change the subject.

I'm not. My arm's dead. She's been asleep on it. Michelle's asleep on my arm. Fancy that.

She's not Becky though.

Will you please shut up, I just want to go back to sleep.

Not much point now, it's almost time to get up.

"Hmm," Michelle whispered in her sleep, rubbing her body against mine.

Look, you're getting an erection. You're going to fuck her again. You never listen to a word I say.

I do so listen.

When did you last listen to me?

That time you said I should take some Buttercup syrup for my cough. I ended up having my stomach pumped.

Only because you spilt the entire bottle down the sink and Mum caught you trying to drain the last bit out of the bottle. I merely suggested you take some medicine, not that you pour it all down the sink. And anyway, you were only six, I hadn't properly developed a sense of my own identity.

My arm's really starting to get really sore now.

Stop, you'll wake her up.

But my arm, if I can just slide it from under her head it won't feel so dead and then I can turn over and go to sleep.

You won't sleep. You're feeling too guilty.

I am not feeling guilty.

Are too. You've had sex. That's a sin you know.

Only if you do it properly.

"Hmmmm." Michelle said, wrapping an arm around me.

Trapped!

You're going to fuck her again.

I might do. I like her. I really do.

How well do you know her?

I've known her for years. Since we played kiss and catch as eight-year-olds.

That's right, I remember now. You tried to kiss her and she ran away crying. What does that tell you?

That she was shy.

She let Alun kiss her and she showed his brother David her knickers. They were blue.

Now you're just getting perverted, shut up.

Look, there's the erection. Told you. Don't listen to me. Don't know why I bother. You're going to get her pregnant or catch HIV or something and it'll serve you right. It'll…

"Hi," I whispered, as Michelle opened her eyes and smiled at me.

"Hi," she kissed me and I kissed her back. Okay, so I wanted to be with Becky but I couldn't be and I was with Michelle and she was naked and felt really nice and all girlie and feminine and her hand was moving down my body and she had a smile that wasn't remotely innocent…

The sex was good as well. I threw myself into it, partly because she was Michelle and very, very attractive and also because if I gave her body my full, undivided attention my subconscious couldn't get a word in edgeways.

At least for a while.

Twenty years later, I was fat and old and working as a teacher in my old school, Campion. As Campion High School had been torn down just after I'd finished and replaced by a housing estate, I couldn't help thinking that getting a job there was a little odd. I wasn't a very good teacher and everyone laughed at me. History was my chosen subject and all the kids thought I was rubbish and my clothes kept vanishing. The worst kid in my class was Geoff Bullion. He was the son Jez had with Becky after they married. Jez spent most of their marriage carrying on with other women and Becky had had a terrible few years. Every time I saw her at parent-teacher evenings she looked at me as if it was my fault, and it probably was. Michelle lost her figure after having the sextuplets and, as I grew to know her, I realised that I really didn't like her after all. What's more, she had grown to hate me with a passion. There was another kid in my class I hated. He sat at the back and threw things at me. I should've given him detention or stabbed him or something but couldn't because his name was William Cade and he kept telling me that the last twenty years were all my fault and if I hadn't slept with Michelle, none of it would've happened. If I'd been honest with Michelle, she wouldn't have become pregnant and Becky would have taken me back and we'd have all lived happily ever after. Apart from Geoff Bullion, who would never have existed. And no one liked him anyway.

"I could stay here forever," Michelle whispered, snuggling up to me in bed.

"Hmm," I replied, thinking that truth might not be called for on this occasion. Mainly because the truth would entail me saying 'Listen, I really don't want to stay because I've decided that I don't like you after all and made a very big mistake and by the way, are you on the pill?'"

"I saw you looking at me, you know," Michelle smiled, sliding up even closer.

"What?" I questioned, a little surprised but trying to make it sound like I didn't actually hear her.

"Last night, when you first came into the house. I saw you looking at me straight away."

"Oh, right," I replied, adding a "Yeah" for good measure.

Reality check.

Michelle was the only person I didn't talk to about Becky the whole fucking party. It struck me as odd that she could think I spent all night staring at her when I was totally oblivious to her presence until we started kissing.

"I always knew we'd end up together," she added.

Until recently I'd spent most of my life dreaming about Michelle saying those words. She was one of the most beautiful women I'd ever met. Most men in town would be more than willing to find themselves with Michelle using her tongue to draw little circles around their left nipple. Not to mention to have done all the things we'd done the previous night. I'd had amazing sex with a beautiful woman I'd spent most of my life dreaming about.

So why couldn't I shake an urge to go home, eat pizza and watch some TV?

Becky.

The voice in my head wouldn't go away. I couldn't shake the feeling that I was somehow being unfaithful to Becky.

But Becky didn't love me. She didn't even like me very much.

"…anything?" Michelle asked, resting on her elbows and smiling.

I had the vague idea that she wanted to have sex again.

"A cup of tea'd be nice," I asked politely.

She seemed totally unfazed by this and leapt out of bed.

"You stay here, you're probably worn out from last night… and this morning. I'll make you a nice cuppa. Help you to get your strength back."

She's got a lovely bum, the demon part of my brain smiled.

It's not Becky's.

Please, stop arguing. This is serious business. When she comes back she's going to expect me to have sex with her.

So?

Well, I don't know if I want to.

She does look good though.

A Manchester United top! She's wearing a Manchester United top!!

And she still looks sexy in it!

Help.

She'd gone into the kitchen. That gave me a few moments alone. I needed an angle on this. I could remember everything from the previous night. We'd had sex twice, no, three times. Unprotected sex… and again that morning. I needed to find out whether she was on the pill. Not an easy question to ask and I definitely wasn't going to have sex with her again. No matter what.

"Tea. Earl Grey," she said, climbing back into bed and cuddling up close, thus making it rather awkward for me to drink the tea she'd just made. Not that it was that nice. There was no sugar in it, not enough milk and I fucking hated Earl Grey. Tasted like perfume. Give me PG Tips any day. Not that I condoned the use of chimpanzees in their adverts.

"Hmm, you're lovely and warm," she purred, stroking my chest with her hand.

"Nice tea," I lied. "Just how I like it."

Maybe I was gay. That would explain things. Maybe I was a closet homosexual and that was why I didn't want to fuck Michelle again.

Having said that, I really didn't fancy the idea of snogging a bloke – even a good-looking one. Not to mention doing the sort of thing Jimmy's told me goes on in those circles.

Becky.

Shut Up.

I conjured up a deep pit in my subconscious and threw the name Becky in it, covering the whole thing with cement and a big fuck-off barbed-wire fence so the name couldn't get out.

When you sleep with someone by accident and they really like you but you decide you don't like them, how long should you stay with them before you can leave and get on with your life?

It was one of the things they should teach you in school. That, and exactly how difficult it was to get a girl pregnant and how you could ask her if she was on the pill without sounding like you were shallow and scared of commitment.

I held onto the mug for a while and looked down at Michelle as she rested on my chest. Okay. I was going to have to talk to her soon. There was only so long I could get away with "Hmmm" and "Cool" before it got repetitive and awkward.

Conversation topics. There must be things we could talk about that didn't entail me bearing my soul. I knew that's what you were supposed to do after sex, but I only liked doing that with people I felt at ease with.

Like Becky.

Damn, the pit wasn't big enough.

Okay, things to talk about. I prepared a quick mental list of possible topics.

1. Geoff. Not a good idea.
2. Becky. Don't think they get on.
3. Hope you're not pregnant.
4. Do you sleep with many men? Only I didn't wear any

condoms and I'm now worried that I might have a sexually transmitted disease.

5. Nice tea.

We'd already done that.

"Looks like it's going to rain," I said, with a smile.

Smiles were good in situations like that. Reassuring.

"Probably," she replied, looking straight into my eyes with that look women get at certain times.

She does have nice breasts, I'll give her that, I thought.

And it wasn't like I was cheating on anyone. Whatshername said she didn't love me and they said the best way to recover from a fall is get back on the bike and start riding again and there I was with the chance to ride a perfectly good bike.

And the way she was slowly moving against me was definitely not a bad feeling.

If I didn't have sex with her again, I was just going to have to lie here and talk to her for a while.

Sex or talking…

Sex or talking…

Sex or talking…

I kissed her and she kissed back.

Hell, if you're in a candy store, why not enjoy yourself while you can?

Before too long, we were rolling around and touching each other in all the right places. I was mostly thinking about Liverpool's chances in their next league game when I slid down to use my tongue. Judging by the way she started to move and her fingers grabbed my hair, she enjoyed herself. The whole thing for some reason made me think of pizza. I'd not had a good pizza since… well, I refused to remember the last time I'd had a good pizza, but I hadn't had one all year. I thought about calling Jimmy up and treating him to one later that day.

Hold it, my mind thought, *you're having sex with a beautiful woman and you'd rather be having pizza and a chat with your mate? That doesn't bode well for the future of this relationship.*

If I'd been honest, I'd have stopped, lifted my head up from between her legs and explained the situation to her.

"Listen, this just isn't working for me so why don't we call it a day? It's alright, I can see myself out."

Even I wasn't that shallow. And my dad always said you should always finish what you've started. Though I'm pretty sure he didn't mean cunnilingus.

Anyway, it didn't matter. I was having sex with a beautiful woman I'd spent most of my life trying to get and I was just going to have to make the best out of it. Whether I wanted to or not.

I decided I should just get it all over with so I could go home and have a proper cup of tea. A few minutes later, I did just that.

"That was great," Michelle smiled, stroking my hair with her hand and starting to ramble on about something.

I looked at her closely. She was pretty. Very pretty, but there were no emotions inside me. I didn't feel anything for her. Already the post-shag guilt was growing stronger.

"I never knew why Geoff and Jeremy had it in for you," she said. "Guess they were just jealous."

"Really?" I said, finding myself intrigued for the first time by what she had to say.

"It was funny, that night you were sick over Geoff. He was

so mad!"

"Yeah, well, I'd rather forget that."

"I can understand," Michelle smiled. "Especially with the way they beat you up the next day. I thought that was so out of order. I tried to stop them but they just wouldn't listen to reason."

I was half dozing again by that point. Maybe… *hold it*, my brain yelled, *did she just say something about Jez and Geoff beating me up?*

"I thought it was dead noble of you not to try and get them back or anything. Geoff was a little worried afterwards. Especially when he found out those men from the pub wanted to find the people responsible."

"Hold it a sec," I spluttered. "Rewind. Geoff and Jez were the cunts who mugged me?"

"Yeah, and I mean it, you were so cool turning the other cheek. Especially with a few of his mates calling you a coward and everything. I knew you weren't, and even if you are, who cares?"

"I didn't know," I said, moving out of the bed and putting on my trousers.

"What do you mean?" Michelle asked.

Bless her. Suddenly the sex-filled tedium of the last twelve hours seemed worth it.

"I didn't know they were the bastards who did me over. Until you mentioned it, I couldn't remember a thing, now…"

Now it was all crystal clear. I could feel the thump from behind, see them kicking me while I was down on the ground. Again and again… like it was happening there and then. The fear I'd been living since it happened was with was replaced with a cold fury.

"Billy, what's wrong? I thought we…" Michelle started to say.

My head snapped round and I stared at her. It was probably the most brutal I'd ever looked in my life. I wasn't seeing Michelle. I was seeing Geoff and Jez. I was seeing them at sixth form. Heads of the pack who used to jump weaker kids, pull their trousers down and black their balls with shoe polish, the thugs who used to spit on my mate 'cause he was Sri Lankan. The heroes of the school just because they could kick a rugby ball. Anger filled me. Anger at everything. I was sick of this fucking town and I was sick of myself. I was sick of fitting into things. I was sick of Billy Cade, the guy with no worries. I was sick of not having Becky. I was sick of drinking. I was sick of the whole fucking thing.

I didn't say a word to Michelle. If words had come out they wouldn't have been good ones. I didn't want to hurt her, but I knew I wouldn't see her again.

At least not naked.

"I've got to go," I said.

I would finish with her but I'd do it properly, not in a fit of anger.

"Billy," Michelle shouted from the doorway. "Call me. Please."

I didn't reply.

Bullion's home number was in the book.

"Listen, you fuck. I know what you did. I'm going to get you. I'm going to cut your fucking balls off with a blunt razor and stick them in your mouth. I'm going to smash both your fucking legs and beat the living shit out of you. Got that?"

"Who is this?"

"Sorry, Mrs Bullion. Wrong number."

"Becky."

"Billy? I don't want to talk to you."

"Please, just listen. It's not about us. I was an idiot. I'm sorry if I hurt you. I didn't mean to. I didn't do anything with Lil, but that's all history now. Are you still seeing Bullion?"

"No." Her voice sounded strange. I tried not to listen to it too closely. I didn't want the anger to go away.

"Do you know where he is? I need to… talk to him."

"You sound strange, Billy. What's wrong?"

That fucker beat me up and now I'm going to kill him.

"Nothing. I'm fine. It's just… personal. So why did you split up?"

"We… Listen, you should know this. He only told me a few nights ago. When you got mugged, it was him and Geoff who did it."

"I know. That's why I want to talk to him. Michelle says Geoff's away until Sunday but I figure Bullion's probably about now."

"You and Michelle seemed to be enjoying the party," Becky said, a little coldly.

The anger was still in me, but talking to Becky was slowly diminishing it. I couldn't let that happen.

"It was just one of those things. Turns out she's not my type after all. Now, Bullion…"

"He's with Geoff," Becky replied, sounding a little happier

and more worried at the same time. "They've gone away to Ibiza for the week on some stag do. They're coming straight back for the match next Sunday."

"The match. Of course. Thanks."

"Billy, don't be a hero…"

I put the phone down in a haze.

Seventeen

Premature, Hospital, Tears

"William…William… are you awake?"

Uh?

"William."

Someone was calling from far away. It sounded like my mum's voice but it couldn't be, it was the middle of the night.

"William, wake up. Doris has been taken to hospital. She's having the baby."

"Can't be, it's not due for another month…" I slurred, turning over and trying to go back to sleep.

Someone flicked on the light.

"That's just it," Mum said. "She's a month premature and apparently there's complications. Your dad sounded worried."

Alarm bells started to ring in my head. I didn't want to ask the next question.

"What kind of complications?"

"He wouldn't say. You know what your father's like. I said I'd go over to the hospital. I was hoping…"

"Of course, give me a second. Have you ordered a cab?"

"One's on its way. I'll meet you downstairs. We've got to pick some things up from your father's place, he thinks she might be in for a while."

My mum scurried off and I dressed before her words sank in.

Doris was having the baby. But she couldn't be. It wasn't due for five or six weeks. That wasn't good.

Downstairs, I was more than a little amazed by the sight that greeted me. My mum had changed. There was no sign of panic, well, maybe a little sign, but for the most part she was organised, efficient and ready for action. It was an emergency and I'd forgotten how well she worked in emergencies.

"Got the spare set of keys?" she asked.

This was a little bit of a surprise. I didn't know Mum knew Dad had given me a spare set of keys to his house. I just nodded as someone knocked on the door. Five minutes later we were both entering Dad's dark and empty house. I couldn't help feeling like a trespasser. Almost like I was spying on Dad's world. Mum stopped for a moment just inside the doorway. It was the first time she'd ever set foot inside.

"It's not as bad as I expected," she muttered to herself. "Not sure about the curtains though."

We both fell silent for a moment and took in the house. It was eerily silent.

"Right," Mum said. "According to your dad, the bedroom's at the top of the stairs. They should have packed a suitcase. I had one ready for three months before you and Jenny were born. Course you two just slipped out. Guess I was lucky. Surprised we didn't have more. We tried. We used to be unstoppable when we first got married."

"Mum…" I said, looking away and hoping to stop her chain of thought right there.

Despite the cleanliness of the house – or maybe because of it – the rooms felt like something torn from a Protestant's Ideal Home exhibition circa 1950 with a little help from IKEA. It turned out there was a suitcase half-packed but Mum decided that a few little extras were needed.

There wasn't much for me to do so I just wandered a little aimlessly around the room trying to take it all in. I was checking his bedside cupboard, not really looking for anything, when I found it.

The Porn.

Quite a lot of porn too. Bondage mostly. Nothing I'd describe as hardcore but definitely not the kind of thing I'd have expected to find on top of my dad's bedside cabinet. Pictures of people dressed in leather, tied up and bent over into, well, into all sorts of positions. I looked up at the bed and, without any permission, the image of Doris and my dad dressed in leather popped into my head and refused to leave.

"Well, I never. I thought he'd packed in that sort of thing years ago," I heard my mum say behind me.

I decided to build a big pit and throw her words into it.

"Are you alright, dear?" she smiled. "Only you've gone all red."

"We should get going," I said, closing the door on my dad's not-so-secret porn stash. "The cab's waiting."

"Yes, dear, and I wouldn't want you to get any more

embarrassed or you might have a heart attack," she laughed.

"We were young once, you know," she added, as I carried the suitcase down the stairs. "We used to get up to all sorts. I remember this one time in New Brighton…"

"Mum, I really don't want to know."

"Very well, dear. But you might've learned something."

Then we were in the cab heading for the hospital. We didn't talk much. They'd taken Doris to Summerdale.

The hospital Jenny died in.

Hospitals are filled with memories. Unfortunately, most of them are bad. At least for me. I hate them. I really do. There's something about the clinical smell and the looks of hope and desperation on the patients that just remind you that this is how we're all going to end up. If we're lucky. We could go in a car crash, a weird gardening accident or just get leukaemia and waste away slowly and painfully.

Mum was amazing. I was putting a brave face on it but she was in total charge. We rushed through the hospital's corridors, only stopping when we caught sight of Dad. He was sitting on his own staring into space, looking older and more tired than ever.

He lifted his head and saw us standing there. He tried a weak smile but was all out of them. For a moment, the years separated them – a barbed wire fence around a minefield.

"This is bloody stupid," Mum cursed, sitting next to Dad and giving him a big hug.

He started to sob softly.

"I love her, Hildie, I really do. I don't want to lose her."

"You won't lose her," my mum smiled. "She's a strong woman, Doris. I can tell."

"How…?" my dad stuttered, wiping tears from his eyes.

"Well, she's put up with you for three years and that takes some doing," she joked, bringing the faintest of smiles to Dad's face.

"You two didn't need to come, you know. I realise Doris isn't… well…"

"Where else would we be?"

The devil in my head suggested that I could be asleep in bed but I refused to listen to it.

"How is she?" Mum asked.

"I don't know. They said she was as well as could be expected but that… well, that seems like hours ago now and no one will tell me anything."

"We'll soon see about that. William, wait here with your father."

Mum marched off in search of answers.

"She seems to be in good form," Dad said.

"Yeah, she is," I answered, suddenly realising that Mum had been better of late. *Really* better. What's more, I hadn't seen her drunk since my mugging.

"Mum's right. She'll be fine," I mumbled, struggling for conversation.

"Wish I still smoked," he stated, staring at his hands.

I wanted to tell him that I loved him and that it would all be okay, but I couldn't. Guess I was just too Northern for that sort of revelation. So instead I offered to get him a cup of tea.

Sometimes words don't matter. When things go badly wrong, the company's more important. There's no need to speak. The very act of being there means the other stuff doesn't need to be said.

"Okay," Mum replied, storming back into the waiting area, leaving a befuddled doctor in her wake. "They wouldn't tell me much but I told them I worked at a school and they opened up a bit. I think they somehow got the impression I was Doris' sister, anyway, the point is they reckon she's out of danger but because of some problems – women's problems – they've decided it's best to get the baby out sooner rather than later. It's a month premature but they don't think there's anything wrong with it. They have babies in here now that are born two or even three months premature and they grow up to be fine."

"Thanks," Dad said, tears starting to cloud his eyes again.

"Now," Mum asked, "who wants a nice cup of tea? I spotted a machine around the corner."

The tea went without any of us paying it much attention. Everything was unreal. It wasn't my life. I'd left that at the door. And when I left the hospital, one way or the other, it wouldn't be the same life. I'd have a new sister or brother or…

I stopped the chain of thought there and then. One sister was enough to lose. Surely the chances…

"More tea?" I asked, needing the act of walking to the machine more than an actual drink of melted plastic and water. Every now and then one of us would smile weakly at the other, who'd smile back and say something like "It'll be all right." For the most part we just sat there in silence, with nurses and doctors and the world rushing by. The darkness outside changed to light somewhere along the way. I glanced up at the clock to check and it said seven fifty-nine. I watched the seconds pass, almost hypnotised as they turned and then clicked in to eight.

Tick. Tock. Tick. Tock.

William Cade, you have a sister. Life is good.

William Cade, she didn't make it. Your father's having a heart attack because of the news and your mother's going back to the bottle. Life sucks. Have fun.

"Anyone want any food?" I asked, as someone walked by with a tray. I wasn't really hungry but it seemed to make a change from asking anyone if they wanted a cup of tea.

"Get your father something. He needs to keep his strength up."

"I'm not hungry," he replied, looking drawn and exhausted.

"I'll get something for him," I said, moving to my feet. "And I'll try and see if there's any more news."

A short while later, I was about to leave the cafeteria with an egg butty for my dad when I caught sight of John sitting on his own at a table with just a cup of tea.

"John, what are you doing here?" I asked.

"Hi, Billy. Just popped in to see Charlie and… another friend."

"Charlie's in here? Is he all right?"

"He'll live. Stupid fucker. You missed all the fun last night. He decided to dump Lil, didn't he?"

"Really?"

"Yeah. Only he was worried that if he did it somewhere

private she'd try and kill him…"

"So?"

"So he did it in the Hope. Told her a few home truths. Very loudly. For what it's worth, she gave as good as she got, and also told him she made all the moves on you and you didn't want anything to do with her. She started crying after that. A lot of people heard her, but thought nothing of it. Well, it's a domestic – you'd have to be an idiot to get stuck in between those two."

I smiled weakly and nodded.

"So he tells her that he doesn't want to see her again and before he knows what's happening, she's got him pressed against the corner of the pub with a pool cue squashed against his neck, screaming 'What do you mean, you don't love me?'

"At that point a couple of the lads tried to drag her off him – on the grounds that Charlie was starting to turn blue and we need him for the match on Sunday. They managed to get her off but she gets free and attacks him again, this time smashing the pool cue over his head and doing something with her hand and his balls – or ball – that makes my eyes water just thinking about it. They're still not sure if they'll manage to save his remaining testicle."

"You mean she ripped it off?" I asked.

"Nearly. We just got her off him before she could tear it free – but there was lots of blood, and poor Charlie's voice. I've never heard a sound quite like it."

"Shit."

"Just thought I'd check up on him."

"Well, at least he's got rid of her at last."

"Don't be stupid. When I saw him ten minutes ago he was

crying and saying how much he loved her and wanted her back. Tosser. So what are you doing here?"

"My dad's having the kid."

"Must be painful."

I smiled politely at the terrible joke.

"It's his wife that's having the kid. Only it's a month early."

"That's nothing," John said. "I was two months premature and weighed three pounds. I was on one of those machines for two months with some virus. The doctor told my mum I was never going to be that big or healthy."

"Honest?" I asked.

"Gospel. Would I lie?" He stared at his tea for a minute.

"How's your mum handling it all?"

"She's with Dad right now. It's amazing, she's been like... well, like a new woman."

John smiled. For some reason the smile worried me a little.

"She's a good woman. I remember when we were at school, she could always take care of herself – and anyone else for that matter. Don't think I ever saw her lose an argument. I remember..."

John looked up, and I could've sworn he was blushing a little.

"How are you holding up? I know this is where, well... you know..."

"Fine," I mumbled. "You okay, you seem a little thoughtful about something?"

"Just thinking about things. I've not been here since my dad died a few years back. Didn't think it'd bother me but it brings it all back, you know?"

I didn't answer. For a second I had a flashback of coming in here years ago with Mum and Dad when we were waiting for news of Jenny. When we hoped, believed, she'd pull through and be okay.

"Yeah, guess you do," John said.

"Listen, you take care, I should get back."

"No problem. Give your mum my best," he said, as I was moving away from the table.

I tried my best to get the sandwich back to my dad before it got cold, but all the corridors looked the same and, within a few moments of leaving the café, I was totally lost.

It took me a few more wrong turns before I had to stop and ask directions.

"Sure," a nurse replied. "It's not that far. In fact, if you cut through the children's ward and take a right and then second left you won't have to go all the way back to reception."

"Cheers," I smiled, turning to follow her directions, only to freeze in front of the doors. It was the ward Jenny had died in. The world around me vanished and I was back there, with my mum crying and my dad cursing and me waiting for her to wake up and tell us all she was only kidding. That was the worst. Seeing her just fade into nothing. There was a change. One second she was my sister and the next she was gone. Just flesh and bone. The days before had been bad as well. The days when part of our brains were already starting to acknowledge the truth, whether we wanted to or not. There was nothing we could do. Nothing but just watch her fade away.

I couldn't go in. I couldn't.

I was about to try and find another way when the door opened.

"It'll be fine," a little girl's voice said, almost making me pass out with shock.

For an instant I really did think it was Jenny.

"Whatever you worry about, you shouldn't, because things always work out. If you worry too much it makes you ill," she explained.

I blinked. It wasn't Jenny. Just someone the same age. Or the age she was when she… when she'd been in the ward.

"You visiting someone?" she asked.

"My dad," I replied. "His wife's having a baby."

"Wow," she grinned. "I've always wanted a kid sister."

"Why are you here?" I asked, half expecting her to say leukaemia.

"I had an asthma attack," she said. "But I'm fine now. The doctor said I can go home later and that I've been very brave."

"You sure look brave," I smiled.

We stood there for a while just looking at each other.

"You're funny," she giggled.

"What?" I asked.

"You're funny. You look all worried and stuff but you're about to have a kid sister. There's nothing to worry about."

"There's always stuff to worry about," I mumbled.

"You're just saying that 'cause you're a grown-up," she pouted.

"I'm not a grown-up!" I replied. "That's a really horrid thing to call someone."

She giggled behind her hand. Her giggle reminded me of Jenny's.

"You going to stand there all day?" she asked. "Or you going to see if you've got a little sister yet?"

"I guess I should go and check, shouldn't I?"

"I think so, or you'll probably get in trouble. I'm always getting in trouble."

"Me too," I smiled. "You take care."

"I will. Bye, Billy," she said, skipping off down the corridor.

"Bye…" I replied. "Hey, how did you know my name?"

But by then she was gone, leaving me outside the ward with a cold egg butty in my hand.

"She's right, this is stupid," I mumbled to myself, walking through the door.

The nurse's directions had been spot on and in no time at all I was walking towards my folks.

Only by then, everything had changed.

My dad was sitting on the chair, hands over his eyes, my mum next to him with her arm wrapped around him.

Both were crying.

My heart sank and my vision clouded.

"What's wrong?" I asked.

It was only when they raised their heads and I saw the expressions of joy that I relaxed. I felt something on my cheeks and realised that I was crying as well.

"She's had the baby," Mum stated simply, wiping the tears away.   "It's a girl. A beautiful baby girl."

The next few days were a blur. A good blur. They kept Doris and the baby in hospital for routine checks. It freaked us all out at first, Dad especially, seeing the poor thing in an incubator, small and pink and all alone. She was alive though, and that was the main thing. It was weird spending so much time at the hospital. Mum started having long chats with Doris. It looked like they were bonding, Mum giving Doris all sorts of tips on how to take care of the baby and volunteering both of us as babysitters should the need ever arise. Dad was starting to look increasingly worried. Now that he didn't have to worry about the baby dying, he could spend time terrified about just how close Doris and Mum were growing. After all, he had divorced Mum to get away from her – and now she seemed to be becoming friends with his new wife. Jimmy came along with us each day. I popped in to see Charlie, but he'd already signed himself out. According to Lee, he was trying to woo Lil back.

It was four days before the reality of it all really hit me.

I had a kid sister.

A kid sister!

I spent a morning at Jenny's grave, telling her about it all. Jenny said she was chuffed. One morning, I was looking at the baby and realised I was always going to be old to her. By the time she left school, I'd be forty. By the time she was my age, I'd be pushing fifty! It was weird but somehow comforting. I spent one night at the Hope talking it all over with Lee and the rest of the time trying to avoid Michelle. I know it was the cowardly thing to do, but I was in a good mood and didn't want to ruin it by breaking up with her, or worse still, giving in to my own personal dark side and sleeping with her again. I didn't want to sleep with her either. I wanted to sleep with Becky, but as I couldn't sleep with Becky (or even talk to her), I'd decided to call the whole thing off and spend some time on my own in the vague hope of finding out who I was.

Saturday night, Jimmy phoned for a chat and, towards the end of the conversation, started to act a little weird. It soon became clear why.

"So you've a match tomorrow," he said, a little hesitantly.

That in itself was odd as he hardly ever talked about football.

"Yeah. Against the Greyhound. If we lose, we're relegated and they win the league. Should be a tough game."

"I was thinking I might come to watch," Jimmy said, taking me a little by surprise.

"What, you come to watch the Hope?"

"Yeah, well, John asked Gabe to play. What with Charlie still being injured and all."

"That's true, I guess after what Lil did to him he has no ball control at all."

"I'll ignore that joke on the grounds that it was terrible."

"Probably a good idea. What's up, you sound like you've got something on your mind?"

"Jeremy and Geoff are playing, aren't they?"

"I should think so," I replied with a smile, knowing where the conversation was leading. "I think they got back from Ibiza today."

"Well, I've been talking with your mum and Becky and we're all a little worried that you might do something stupid."

"Becky was worried about me?"

"Yeah, but don't let it go to your head. She said she wants to be by herself and has had enough of men for a lifetime. Sorry. Anyway, you're still supposedly seeing Michelle and you know what I'm getting at."

"I'm not going to start anything with them. You were right, they're neanderfucks, I can't be arsed with them. I don't even feel pissed off with them anymore. The baby, seeing it in hospital and everything, it's helped me put everything into some kind of perspective."

"Good to hear," Jimmy said.

He didn't believe me. I could tell. But it didn't matter. It was the truth. The baby was alive. I was alive and it was spring and everything was good with the world.

We were going to win the football match as well. No doubt about it.

And Becky was worried about me.

Cool.

Eighteen

The Big Kick-Off

It felt like the FA Cup Final. Jimmy was there as promised – with Becky next to him. I risked a wave to both of them and was chuffed when I got a nervous smile back from Becky.

"Hope you don't mind me asking," Gabriel said as he saw me smiling at Becky, "but Jimmy told me about you and that Michelle girl and I was just wondering if you'd got round to splitting up with her yet?"

"Not really," I said, sounding more than a little guilty. "I've not seen her for over a week, though. I think she's got the idea that it was just a one-night thing."

"That must be why she's come to watch the game then," Gabriel said.

I followed his gaze to just down the touchline from Becky, where a worried-looking Michelle was standing on her own. She waved to me and blew me a nervous kiss.

"Looks like you're getting yourself a regular harem on the go,"

Lee laughed, slapping me on the back.

An uneasy smile crossed my face. Still, it could be worse. Becky looked a little annoyed by Michelle's presence, while Geoff and Jez were having a quiet few words with each other nearby. Their recent trip to Ibiza had left them badly sunburned. They looked so amazingly stupid it was impossible to be mad at them.

Judging by the look on Geoff's face, he was finding it quite easy to be mad at me. I guess someone had just told him about the party.

The rest of the Greyhound were busy warming up. Compared to the players we had, they were athletes. They were stretching and running and passing the ball to each other – just like proper footballers. I looked at our side. Lee was finishing his pre-match fag while one of our midfield maestros was downing a can of Tennant's Extra. If flab counted as skill we'd have been the favourites. Hell, we'd have been unstoppable. As it stood we were doomed. Not that it mattered. There was more to life than football.

I thought of my baby sister and smiled.

They won the toss and decided to swap ends – hoping to wear us out before we'd even started by making us run to the other end of the pitch. It was a good plan. By the time half our team had reached their new positions, two were apparently having minor heart attacks. As I walked by Jez and Geoff, they blocked my path, Geoff placing the palm of his hand on my chest.

"If you're trying to get me worked up, forget it," I tried to explain, noticing both Gabriel and John were suddenly standing behind me. "Whatever problem I had with you guys is history.

Nice tans though."

Okay, so maybe I still hated them a little.

"Are you trying to nick my Michelle?" Geoff said, jabbing a finger into my chest.

I just smiled.

"You fucked it up with Becky. If you mess with Michelle, we'll fucking kill you," Jez threatened.

"You already tried that," I replied. "Like to see you try when I'm sober."

I could feel my peacefulness slipping away.

"At least my mum's not a cheap tart who shags anything that moves," Jez said. "Heard she's got some new tosser in her pants at the moment. Pity the poor bastard. I'd love to meet him, the fucking loser."

"Watch who you're calling a loser," John said. "And that's my Hildie you're bad-mouthing."

"Lads, we've got a game to start," the ref said, beginning to realise it was not going to be a clean game.

Lee and Gabriel had dragged John back into our half of the pitch, Big Mac and his kid brother persuading Jez and Geoff to get in place for the kick-off.

"Excuse me, but you'll need to step back before we start," the ref said, gesturing to me.

I glanced up, but didn't really take in what he was saying. The full implications of John's words were slowly starting to dawn on me. My mum had just joined Becky and Jimmy at the touchline. I glanced back just in time to see John blow her a kiss. She giggled like a schoolgirl and blew one back.

"Hold on a sec. What did you mean by 'my Hildie'? Are you

seeing my mum?"

John flinched. He actually looked boyish and embarrassed. Well, as embarrassed and boyish as a six-foot-six mentally unstable ex-para could look.

"We've been meaning to tell you for months, but between one thing and the other we just didn't get round to it."

"Months?" I muttered, as a whistle went off somewhere.

"Hey, the game's started," he said, looking extremely relieved and rushing off towards the ball. "We'll talk about this later, yeah?"

"You've been seeing her for months?" I shouted, running after him and completely ignoring their number seven who was running towards me with the ball.

"Billy, get with the programme!" Gabriel shouted.

I turned, saw their player, tackled him and belted the ball upfield before running after John again.

"What do you mean, months? What are your intentions towards her? How did it start? She is my mum, you know?"

"It started just after you got mugged, okay? She's a fine woman – you should be proud of her. And she's got a great body."

"John, please. That's my mother you're talking about."

"Sorry. It's just that I've never felt like this before. Well, not since I was a kid anyway. Watch out, they're back again."

I looked up to see the ball flying towards us both.

"Mine," John said, trapping the ball with his foot and dribbling upfield far faster than he normally would have.

I looked at the touchline only to catch my mum shouting support – not for me, but for John. His run didn't last long. He heard my mum shout something, turned to smile at her and tripped over the ball. Within seconds, the whole of their team were rushing towards us, Geoff leading the charge. He cut free at the edge of our penalty area and tried to run past me. I was about to make a tackle when Gabriel beat me to it.

"I've got him!" he shouted, kicking the ball upfield.

There was no time to argue, as the ball landed straight at the feet of one of their players who belted it straight back towards our goal. I sprinted into the six-yard box to stop it, noticing Jez making a dash in the hope of connecting his head with the ball. It flew over my head to Lee, who belted it up the field to his older brother.

John's shagging my mum. A voice popped up in my head. *I should say something.*

The voice made me oblivious to everything else. Including Geoff's late challenge. Well, I say late, it was more than late as I hadn't touched the ball for five minutes. His elbow smacked into me as I went down.

"You fucking cunt," he whispered, trying to help me up. "Michelle's mine. Okay?"

Before I could get up and give him a good kicking, he was gone.

The baby, I thought. *Focus on the baby. Peace, Love and good happiness stuff.*

I don't need to resort to violence to be better than him.

"Let it go," John said by my side. "We need to win this game. Beating them is far more important than any personal vendettas."

"Yeah," I answered somewhat half-heartedly, turning and running towards the ball. Jez was running for it as well. Actually, he seemed to be running for me rather than the ball. I avoided his challenge and passed the ball to Gabriel. Someone on their side called him a fag but he ignored it and produced a blinding run straight through their centre, whacking the ball straight into the top corner of their net.

We were all ecstatic until we noticed that the referee had blown his whistle and motioned for an offside. Gabriel complained, with good reason, and got booked. While he was complaining, they took the free kick, belted it upfield and scored.

The rest of the first half was more of the same. We had another goal disallowed and a near miss. There was a lot of hard tackling and a couple of punches. Just before half-time, we'd decided that the ref was a tosser when they chipped the ball to their number six. I didn't know the guy's name but I'd already started to acknowledge the fact that he was a good player. I was running back after him as he dribbled the ball on the edge of the penalty area, taking it towards the touchline. For once his control failed him and the ball rolled out for a goal kick. At least that was what everyone thought. The ref blew his whistle and started motioning with his hand.

"What? I never touched it!" I yelled, as Paul, our goalie for the day, begrudgingly rolled the ball out to the corner flag. The ref shook his head and ran towards us, booking Paul for dissent and pointing to the penalty spot.

"What for?" came the automatic response of the whole team.

Their side started to laugh when they realised what was happening. In his defence, the number six tried to tell the ref nothing happened before Jez dragged him away, telling him to keep his gob shut.

Paul managed to get his fingertips to the penalty but the ball still went into the net. On cue, the ref blew for half-time. There were still a few minutes of the first half left but I think he was starting to fear for his own safety, as someone had mentioned that John and Lee used to be paras.

The thought hit me that not only were we about to be relegated but the two people I hated most in the world were about to get championship medals. The day was not going as planned. Maybe I *was* being too nice. We managed to make it to one of the nets and spent a few minutes slagging the ref off and a few more generally whinging about the total unfairness of life.

"Listen, we can still turn this around," I said, in between trying to get my breath back. A couple of the team nodded in agreement, a few more lit up their second fag of the break.

"For a start, their front two seem more intent on trying to get me than score."

More nods.

"And Gabriel nearly scored."

"Aye, he's not bad for a gay bloke," someone said.

"Thanks," Gabriel replied. "And you're not bad for a homophobic Northerner."

"Thanks," the guy grinned.

"Billy's right," Lee added. "I reckon we need to hassle them a bit more. Get up and stuck in."

It went on like this for another five minutes. Each of us talking in clichés that we'd picked up from watching too much *Match of the Day.*

As we kicked off the second half, you'd have thought we'd already lost. Things were bad enough, when we suddenly found ourselves down to ten men. I'd ended up with the ball and planned on planting it upfield towards John, who was being hassled by Geoff. As the ball was going towards him, John turned and punched Geoff straight in the face. Geoff went straight down, his nose a mass of blood, and the ref, who'd been right in front of them, rather nervously pulled out a red card. For a second, I thought John was going to pull the ref's head off – I'd never seen him so furious – but then he was marching off the field, making a beeline for me as he went.

"Remember how I said you shouldn't try to have a go at those two cunts?"

I looked back, confused.

"Bullion and the other cunt."

"Yeah…"

"Well, forget what I said. I was speaking out of my arse. You should maim the fuckers."

"What?"

"Let's just say he used some bad language in regard to your mother and leave it at that. Now do me a favour, as soon as you get the chance, kill them. They have it coming."

So much for peace, love and good happiness stuff.

"Billy, what's up?" Lee asked. I explained and Lee's face turned bright red to match his brother's, who was being calmed down by my mum and Becky.

The reason for the sending-off spread through the team like wildfire and within a second of the match starting again, Geoff went down under a crushing challenge from Lee. One the ref decided was fair – probably because he was starting to fear for his own life. It left Geoff with a rather bad limp. I spent most of the game trying to cripple Jez or Geoff. Every time I got near them though, Gabriel was there, making sure there was no way I could foul them. It was bloody annoying. Then my chance came. We had a throw-in back in their half and Geoff was unmarked. I ran towards him, fist ready, only to almost cry when he started to walk from the pitch – substituted! I was crushed. How could they do that before I had a chance to maim him? It just wasn't right. I looked around and saw Jez standing at the near post. At least I could get him. The throw-in was a good one, Gabriel got the ball on the edge of the penalty area and chipped it in towards the goal. I shot forward and found myself with only Jez and the goalkeeper between me and the goal. The ref was nowhere to be seen. This was my chance. I could clobber Jez and get away with it. Of course, I also had the chance of scoring.

To foul or to score, that was the question. Whether it was nobler in the heart to cripple the fucker or to take up the ball and by dribbling, score? Aye, there was the rub.

"Use the Force, William," Alec Guinness said inside my head.

I couldn't work out how that would help me maim Jez, so instead I concentrated on getting the ball and didn't see Jez himself rush in with both legs aimed straight at me. I went down in a heap and was about to smack him when I saw the ref pulling out a red card. I blew Jez a kiss as he left the pitch.

Gabriel made short work of the penalty.

And the crowd went wild. Well, I say crowd, I actually mean Mum, Becky and Jimmy. Michelle started shouting loudly as well, having moved only a few yards away from Becky. I glanced over and saw the two of them have a bit of a slanging match before starting to clap and cheer me with even more enthusiasm.

Each seemed to be trying to outdo the other one. Better still, when Bullion tried to talk to Becky she snapped at him. For a second, I thought he might even start to cry, but that was too much to ask for.

I was starting to feel good. Maybe non-violence was the path to enlightenment after all. I looked towards my mum, John had his arm around her now and she seemed to be really happy. I felt good. With Jez and Geoff off the pitch it got tougher but fairer. Lee, who'd never scored in his life, managed to pull one back thanks to working a wonderful move with Gabriel. When I suggested they made a great team, he started to blush.

At this point, I'd like to say I scored the winner, but I didn't. I did help, though. With a few minutes remaining I gave it the old Cade special – meaning I whacked it blindly upfield. Somehow, Gabriel managed to get on the end of it, passing a couple of their players before scoring. Three-two with only a couple of minutes left. The goal seemed to take the fight out of their side. A few minutes later, the final whistle blew. We'd won. Becky and Mum started singing "We Are the Champions!" from the touchline and I was a little surprised to see John joining in. As everyone went to congratulate Gabriel for his winning goal, I swear I saw Jimmy look a little jealous on the touchline. Especially when Robert, a midfielder, tried to kiss Gabriel full on the lips. This seemed to embarrass Gabriel and he just turned to Jimmy and shrugged his shoulders. I turned from the celebrations and walked over to where Bullion was standing, a few yards away from his teammates, who seemed to be blaming their defeat on his sending-off.

"Jez," I said, in a perfectly calm and rational voice.

"Cade, what the fuck do you want?"

"I just wanted to have one last go at making the peace. No hard feelings, okay?"

"Fuck off, you cunt. Kicking your fucking head in was the best laugh I've ever had."

"Oh come on, just let's forget it, okay? It was a good game."

"Listen, you wanker, why don't you piss off before I beat you up again?"

A silence was descending over the post-match celebrations as the players gathered around us.

"Leave it, Billy," someone said behind me.

"Last time you beat me up, you attacked me from behind. Want to try that again?" I asked, stepping forward.

"Too fucking right," Jez cursed, lunging towards me.

I moved to the left and smacked him in the face with a truly wondrous punch.

Okay, so non-violence might be the path to enlightenment, but I never claimed to be that enlightened – and seeing Jez lying in the mud with what turned out to be a broken nose definitely helped me to achieve a nirvana-like grace.

"You're going to fucking die," he said, scrambling to his feet to attack me. Geoff was about to join him when some large hands grabbed him from behind.

"Now, what was that phrase you used to describe my girlfriend?" John asked.

Geoff went very pale and whimpered as John slapped him across the face.

It was a simple slap carried out by a master of the art. Everyone, my mum included, had gathered around.

"You shagged my bird," Geoff yelled, pointing at me but unable to get by John's outstretched arm.

"Yeah, and mine," Jez added.

"Mine too," someone on our team shouted. "But it's okay, I never liked her much."

"And you puked over my mate," Jez said. "While trying to steal his girl in broad daylight."

"I'm not his girl," Michelle shouted, pushing her way towards me. "And it was night anyway. You don't get broad daylight at midnight. God, you're such a loser!" And with that she tried to kiss me. I say tried to kiss me, because I didn't want to kiss her back.

"Billy, what's wrong?" Michelle asked.

I smiled weakly. This was no good. I had to break up with her. She looked up at me with big blue eyes. Becky's brown ones were far nicer, but these reminded me of a puppy in the rain. Or Bambi. I was going to shoot Bambi.

"Can't you take a hint?" Becky said from beside me. "He's not interested."

"Yeah, right, like he'd rather have some dopey cow like you. Couldn't even satisfy your husband from what I heard. That's why he used to sleep around."

I flinched at the words.

"Michelle, that's not on," I said, but no one was listening to me. They were too busy watching Becky and Michelle fight. Michelle had a definite feminine style – all scratching and hair-pulling – while Becky was more disciplined, probably due to all the boxercise.

"You do realise they're fighting over you?" Jimmy said. He

was totally bemused by the scene – and the expressions on some of the blokes watching them.

"I know," I replied, trying not to smile.

Part of me thought I should do something, but I was having a moment. Becky was fighting over me.

"We should try and stop them," Jimmy said.

"Give it a minute," I replied, smiling as Becky tripped Michelle up, sending her flying into a muddy puddle. "I've never had two women fight over me before."

I didn't get the chance to savour it for much longer, as Becky landed a beautiful uppercut that totally flattened Michelle. For a second we were all a little worried that she might even have killed her. Then Michelle started to cough.

"Nice punch," I smiled.

"Bitch," Becky said under her breath before spinning around to face me.

I smiled. I had to. She looked totally stunning.

"And you can stop grinning as well!" she snapped. "This isn't about you. I've hated that cow since she was eight and nicked my first boyfriend."

"Hey, I never argue with someone who punches like that," I answered, only to see Jez trying to get towards me. Gabriel stopped him with a quick backhand. John looked impressed. Both teams soon started fighting, while the ref and linesmen decided to leg it. The whole thing was getting messy, but Becky and me seemed to be in an oasis of peace in the middle of all the chaos and flying fists. I was vaguely aware that this was because John, Lee and Gabriel were keeping people away from us. Gabriel seemed to be especially enjoying himself.

I smiled at Becky.

"You look a mess," I grinned, wiping some mud from her cheek.

"Flatterer," she smiled back.

"Friends?" I asked.

She remained silent for what seemed like an eternity.

"Sure," she said, looking away and sounding a little disappointed.

"Hey, Gabriel, what's happened to Jimmy?" I asked.

"He's not really into gratuitous violence, so I said I'd meet him later. Excuse me a sec," he said, grabbing one of their players by the throat. "Now, did you or did you not call me a great big mincing queen while we were playing football?"

"Only in a good way," his victim coughed.

I tried not to think about the way him and Lee were bonding. Everyone I knew seemed to be bonding. It was scary.

"You going to be okay or do you need a hand?" I asked, as sirens started to blare.

"Don't be daft. The girl's mad about you, any fool can see that. Go get a drink or something. I can sort this out. Just tell James I'll be a little late. I might have to help them with their questioning."

"Gabriel… this is serious."

"No, it's not, I've got some good friends down the station. These officers might look hard but you haven't seen them the way I have. Now go, before she comes to her senses."

Geoff and Jez were trying to leap over a fence to avoid the police. Jez slipped and looked up to find a truncheon in his face.

"Thanks." I turned to face Becky.

She wouldn't look me in the eyes. It was as though she was worried that if she did, I'd see some truth in hers. I already knew the truth, though. I had for the longest of times. Even when I thought the truth was dead and misery was king.

"So you're mad about me," I whispered, as we left the field.

I tried to make it sound like a joke, but failed. Instead it sounded like a prayer.

Becky smiled nervously.

"You know it really hurt when you dumped me."

"I didn't dump you," she answered. "I just…"

"You said you didn't love me."

"I did, didn't I? Sorry about that."

"No problem," I smiled, as we left the park.

I glanced back to see a dozen or so officers breaking up the fight. Gabriel was talking to one of them, Lee by his side. They all seemed to be getting on well.

"Looks like it's all going to be alright," I said.

"It does, doesn't it…" she smiled.

It was a good smile.

I took a chance and slipped my hand into hers.

"Good job we're just friends," I whispered.

"Yes," she answered, holding my hand tighter.

And for a while we all lived happily ever after.

ACKNOWLEDGEMENTS

Hope you enjoyed the book. Please leave a quick review online at Amazon, Good Reads or one of the many other digital book sites popping up. It's a crowded marketplace and a new book needs all the help it can get to reach a wider audience – and online reviews really do work. A novel takes a lot of time so I want to thank a few people who've helped the creative process. Gary Gilbert and Paul Morris first and foremost. Gary for his usual sterling design work and Paul for the amazing cover art. More thanks go to Melanie Scott for a much-needed editorial assist, and the original readers: Nick Abadzis, Glenn Dakin, John Tomlinson, Dan Rachael, Liv Guy, Corrina Bouch and Helen Bouch. Special thanks go to Stephen Butler, Stephen Norton, Martin Connor, Jimmy Norton, John Gilgannon and Neil Quarterman for help, inspiration and drinks and Tim Quinn for helping me promote *Punch Drunk Kisses* and *Zombie 18*.